Enjoy the book Karen

ADVENTURES GONE SO WRONG

Karen Hillier

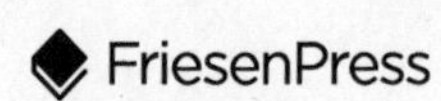

One Printers Way
Altona, MB R0G 0B0
Canada

www.friesenpress.com

First Edition — 2023

Editor, Kayla Schwantz
A special thank you to my daughter Kayla Schwantz for the countless hours she spent editing my book.

ISBN
978-1-03-918735-1 (Hardcover)
978-1-03-918734-4 (Paperback)
978-1-03-918736-8 (eBook)

1. FICTION, CRIME

Distributed to the trade by The Ingram Book Company

Dedication

I dedicate this book to my husband Daryl, who always believes in me and says I can do anything I put my mind to.

In memory of my mom, Laurea Marie Burke. March 22, 1934 – December 16, 2018, whom will always hold a special place in my heart.

I WAKE UP TO the sound of a brisk wind and the chirping of birds. The sound of trucks on the highway can be heard and a beautiful sunrise can be seen, at 6am. The sky is so colorful, that it reminds me of cotton candy. Some mornings, the sky looks like fire with the red and orange colors mixed in. This is what living in the woods in a tiny cabin feels like. For me, it's being able to get out and explore and find things you think you will never find. My heart races when I think about my day and taking any dirt road I can find. It makes me want to get up each morning and head out the door. *I am going to make the best of what I have and live life to the fullest. What will I find in the deep dark woods?* I think to myself.

I make my way to the kitchen to make a pot of coffee, then go outside to get some firewood for my woodstove. Coffee is done, so it's time to go sit on the deck and watch the birds fly around, while listening to the planes flying up above. It's so quiet and calming living in the woods. I sip my coffee and enjoy the scenery. It's peaceful and relaxing, so I don't want to go inside to get dressed. After sitting outside for a couple of hours, it's time to get ready to go for a nice long walk.

I stoke the fire and do my dishes, then get dressed and start out for a nice long walk. I realize I forgot to take my phone, so I head back to grab it. Sometimes, I walk with my neighbor and a friend, but today I'm by myself. I walk for about a kilometre down the dirt road and several big trucks pass by. I continue to walk when I see something in the distance that looks like a dark object. I am trying to get a closer look and realize it is without a doubt, a Big Black Bear. I freeze and think to myself, *just don't move. Don't run, just try to keep still.* Of all times, this is the time when I don't see any traffic coming or going. I think, *if someone is passing by, I will try to flag them down.* The bear has other ideas as he starts to head towards me. Panic sets in, so I start to run as fast as I can, but the bear starts to catch up to me. *This is the end*, I think. *My life is over.* I crouch down instinctively covering my head waiting to feel his teeth and claws ripping through my flesh, when all of a sudden, I feel the rush of wind as he runs past me. I look up to see two deer running through the woods as the bear chases after them instead. I decide that now is my chance to get away and run to a small shack that is close to me. I open the door and quickly slam it shut when I get inside.

I don't remember seeing that shack before while on my walks. I walk that road quite often but I am glad it is here and happy it's open. "No Service" the screen on my phone says. I try and try to move around hoping it changes…but it doesn't.

Inside the shack are tools, some old books and junk. The smell of musty mildew and dust all around, tells me this shack must have been abandoned for many years.

I wait about 2 hours and can't hear anything. Slowly, I open the door and peek out. I don't see the bear or animals near by. I know I need to try to get home, so I get out of the shack and quickly start walking towards my cabin. I am terrified the bear will come back and have me for supper. I startle and freeze every time I hear a noise. I get about halfway home when I come across a few people riding horses. They stop and tell me to be very careful as there has been a sighting of a bear in the area.

"Yes" I say, as I tell them about my encounter with the bear and what happened.

"I ran to a shack back there and hid there for over 2 hours."

"Where do you live?" one of them says.

"Oh, I am just down the road about half a kilometer." I reply.

"Well, you shouldn't be walking alone with a bear on the loose. Climb up here and I will give you a ride home," he says.

I climb up on the horse and get a ride to my driveway. I thank them and tell them to be safe. I can't believe what just happened. That was very close and could have had a very different outcome. I am very lucky.

AS I MAKE MY way up my driveway to the cabin, I notice a tree came down across my roof while I was gone. I go inside to see if there is any damage, but luckily there is none to the inside of the cabin. I call my neighbor and tell him about the tree and he comes over to look.

"I will go home and get a ladder along with a chainsaw and I will be back," he says.

He arrives back with his chainsaw and ladder and puts the ladder against the cabin to climb up and take a closer look. He comes back down to get the chainsaw and climbs back up the ladder to start cutting the tree. Eventually it falls off the roof and on to the ground.

"There is very little damage to the roof. Nothing to worry about!" he says.

"Yay! Thank you" I yell up.

When he comes back down, I thank him once more before he leaves. I go inside and make some supper, then realize I should probably call my neighbor to tell them about the bear in the area and to be careful.

"Well, I see you walking up and down the road all the time, so maybe take a break for awhile" he says.

"I will. I had a close call today and I don't want that to happen again" I respond.

I was so concerned about the tree on my roof that I forgot to tell him when he was over helping. I put more wood in the woodstove and decide to clean up my dishes, then go for a walk around my property as I like to do some evenings.

IT IS VERY MUDDY out, so it's rubber boot weather. I make a cup of hot chocolate and put it in a tall mug with a lid, then I get dressed and venture out around the trails on my property. I come to a real muddy spot where my boot gets stuck in the mud. I can't move or lift my boot at all. I put my cup down on the ground and I try and try but my boot is stuck. So, I decide to pull my foot out of the boot. I can't balance myself on 1 foot, so I need to put my foot down in the mud. It feels weird to have a foot in the mud with only a sock on. I start tugging on the boot until I get it free. Then, I take my muddy sock off and try to knock some mud off my boot so it doesn't get stuck again.

As I go to put my boot back on, I notice a weird looking object in the sole of the boot. I clear the mud away and it is an odd shaped bone that doesn't look like an animal. It is wedged tight between the grooves. I get a stick and start poking around the mud as I snag a piece of clothing. It isn't any clothing of mine that I can tell. I keep poking around and find a few more bones. Some are long, some are small and tiny and others look like broken pieces.

I stop digging any further and call the police to tell them what I have found.

"I was walking around my property when my foot got stuck in the mud. After I removed my boot and cleaned it off, I noticed something in the sole of the boot. Upon further investigation, I came across clothing and other bones." I tell him.

"Can I have your address so we can come take a look for ourselves?" says the officer.

"Sure," I say and give him the address and directions to my cabin.

Within an hour there are 2 police cars that show up to look. I go over to introduce myself and tell them what I found.

"Hello, I'm Officer Clay. Can you show us where you were when this happened?" he says.

"Yes, it's muddy so be prepared," I say with a smile.

I take them to the trail where I found the bones and clothing.

"It doesn't look like animal bones but hard to tell until we get it to the lab. Where are the pieces of clothing you found?" he asks.

"Oh! right over here. I put them aside." I reply.

"Well, these pieces look like they have been here for many years. Can I have your boots to take to the lab? We need to get them analyzed to see what this is" he says.

"Yes, you can have them," I answer.

I go to the cabin to get another pair of boots and put them on. The officer takes my rubber boots and bags them as evidence. They dig around a bit more and pull out more bones.

"How long have you lived here and who did you buy the property from?" asks Officer Clay.

"It is my daughter and husband's property. I just live here in the cabin with my husband. We have only been here for about 3 years" I say.

"Where does your daughter and her family live? "I will need to go talk to them, if they are home," he tells me.

"They just live the next driveway down," I tell Officer Clay.

"Ok, I am going to head over and ask them a few questions, then I will be back," he responds

The other officer starts digging around the mud and pulls up more bones.

"I am not sure what we have here, but it looks like these bones could be human, so I am calling in the forensic team" says the officer with a surprised look on his face.

He has a feeling this is a crime scene. The officer comes back from talking to my daughter and husband.

"They have been living here for about 4 years and will look for the name of who they bought the property from, then get back to us."

"That's good," says the other officer replying to him.

Within an hour, the property is filled with a forensic team of about 10 people. They are carrying cases and tools as they walk to the trail of mud.

"We will be setting up and trying to find out what is on your property. It will take us a few hours to get everything set up and then we will start digging around the mud," Officer Clay says.

"Ok, I will just stay back on my deck and watch from here," I tell him.

"Good idea. We need you to keep your distance and stay away from this area. We must dig up the entire area to see what else is buried and it is getting dark soon" he says.

They set up lights and rope off the area. There is a couple of officers that stay the night so they can continue digging. I am in total shock of what I have discovered on my property. An officer heading back to his patrol car stops to talk with me.

"We will have more officers come back early tomorrow morning to continue the investigation," says the officer,walking away and looking exhausted.

Could it be a body? Who was it and how long has all this been here? I think.

SO MANY QUESTIONS I want answers to. I must wait until they return in the morning to find out more. I go inside and have a bite to eat, then get ready for bed. I know I won't be able to get any sleep. I sit out on the deck for hours looking at the lights they set up. I can hear them talking, but can't make out what they are saying. I need to go inside to try to catch a few hours sleep. I know morning is not far away and it is going to be a long day. I just want them to come back and get this dealt with. I am hoping it is a mistake and just an animal, not human remains.

At about 7am, I get dressed and make coffee. As I sit out on the deck, I watch more officers arrive. I now know that things are more serious than I imagined. A few hours go by when more people are coming in. I can see them lay a tarp on the ground and put stuff on it. I think, *this can't be good. They must be finding other items or bones.* Finally, an officer comes down to where I am sitting on my deck.

"We have discovered human remains buried in the mud," one of them yells.

"Wow" is all I can say.

"We are not sure of who or how many bodies we are talking about," says the officer.

I am in complete shock to think there is a body, or multiple, on the trail I walk so often.

A few more hours go by and Officer Clay comes to tell me there are at least 2 bodies buried here. "They are not too far from each other but have been here for quite sometime," he says. They continue with their digging all day and into the early evening. They are satisfied there are only 2 bodies buried here. They need to go to the station and look for missing persons that were never found. They also need to wait for the body parts to be sent for determination of the cause of death and how long they might have been here. We all hope they can I.D. the bodies and at least give families closure for their loved ones.

One month later...

As I am enjoying my first coffee of the day, my phone rings. The lead investigator is calling to update me on the case. "I am informed it was 2 young females found on the property and they have been there for over 20 years" he says.

They need to continue investigating who lived on the property years ago and try to track them down for any information they may have.

Two months later...

Another month goes by, before I get another call updating me about the 2 bodies found on my property. Upon further investigating and contact with the families they got more information. They were 2 girls, both still in high school and heading in different directions after graduating; they decided to travel together for a summer vacation and backpacking. Their families lost contact with them and they were never heard from again.

I want to know more about the girls and who they were. I need to find out why this happened. I start looking up missing persons but don't have any luck finding answers. I keep thinking, *what did these girls go through and how did they die? Who did this and why? Did they suffer?* All these questions with no answers. I cant imagine what the family has felt for so long. I am not about to let this go. I need answers and their families deserve them.

This is hard to believe these girls have laid here buried all this time. I keep thinking *if I didn't find them, they may never have been found.* I am glad I went for a walk that evening in the mud. The families can finally have closure.

Wow many times in the last 3 years have I walked that trail and right over top of those graves? I think.

I want to do something to give the girls a memorial for where they were found, so I decide to plant 2 trees where the bodies were laid for so long.

Four months later...

It has been four months to the day, since the girls were found. My phone rings and it's Officer Clay, the one who was on scene that night.

"We have been in contact with the families of the 2 girls found on your property. The moms of the 2 girls, are wondering if they can come to the place where the girls were found. I am calling to ask if this would be something you would allow them access to," he tells me.

"I would love to meet them! Please pass along my number and they can call me whenever they are ready," I immediately respond.

After a few days, I receive a call from one of the moms. We talk on the phone for over an hour. She asks so many questions about how I had found the girls. I ask a lot of questions too and want to know more about who the girls were. The mom tells me the girls were best friends just trying to figure out who they were. They both loved to travel and they wanted to finish school and graduate together. After over an hour of talking we say goodbye and she says she will contact me when they plan on coming to the property. I hope this will give them closure.

I am very excited, yet scared at the same time to meet them. I know it will be a very emotional time but is needed to help them heal. These families need answers and maybe coming here will help with that.

I wake up this morning to my phone ringing. I answer and it is the mom of the other victim.

"Hi" says the lady on the other end.

"My name is Rhonda and I am one of the mothers of the girls found on your property."

She catches me off guard as I am just waking up, so it takes me a second to realize what she has said.

"OH! Hi Rhonda, my name is Jill. I am so glad you reached out to me and so sorry for your loss," I say softly.

"At least now, we can have closure" says Rhonda.

"This has been a long time waiting, to finally hear the news that the girls have been found. We prayed everyday they would be found alive" she says.

"I am sure this has been a shock to all of you. I am thankful they have been found and I hope you can all have some closure" I say.

"Yes, we can now lay them to rest with the help of you. We can not thank you enough and appreciate you meeting with us. If it's ok with you, we would like to come visit in a week. Would Wednesday next week work for you?" asks Rhonda.

"That is fine. If you have a pen, I will give you directions to get here. I live in the woods, so you will need to know how to find my place" I tell her.

"Great! I have a pen and paper, so go ahead with the directions," she says.

Rhonda writes the directions down and we talk a little bit more about the upcoming visit. I am very excited to meet and help these families. I hope it will give them the opportunity to have peace of mind. After talking for over an hour, she says goodbye and tells me she will see me soon.

I make a phone call to the police to ask if it is ok to take down all the tape around the property before the families arrive. I don't think it should be something they should see when they arrive here. I am told to take it all down as they are done, so I spend the day cleaning up and removing all the yellow tape surrounding a large area of my property. I fill in some of the hollow holes where they were digging. I think to myself, *how this would look if I arrived and this wasn't done?* It starts to look like my property is getting back to normal. I do as much as I can in the short time that I have. I put everything in large garbage bags and drag it back to the cabin, then I take it all to the dumpsters. *Out of site, out of mind,* I think. It has been a long time, waiting for this day to come.

It is time to head inside and make some supper. I put a piece of chicken in my air fryer and make a tossed salad. I eat and decide I should make something for when the families arrive the next day, so after supper, I cut up some cheese and meat, then bake a cake and a loaf.

I watch some tv, before going to sit on the deck with a cup of tea. The stars are out and it is a beautiful night. My mind is racing thinking about tomorrow and meeting both moms. I head inside to try to get some sleep. I know it will be hard to sleep, but I have to try.

I toss and turn but manage to get a few hours of sleep. I wake at about 6am, make coffee and head to the deck. The birds are chirping and the sky is just starting to get bright. I know it is going to be a long and stressful day.

I go inside at about 8am and get dressed, before making some breakfast. After breakfast, I go for a nice long walk, while anxiously awaiting their arrival. I know they will be here in the next few hours. I am nervous, but excited at the same time.

THREE HOURS LATER, A small black car pulls in into the driveway. I walk over to greet them as they get out.

"Hi Jill, I was so nervous when I called to talk before, that I forgot to tell you my name is Kay" says the first mom who I spoke with on the phone.

We hug and we talk for a bit on the deck. I make a pot of coffee and we have some snacks that I prepared the day before. They have pictures of the girls with them, so we look through old photos of them. They were 2 beautiful girls that didn't get to enjoy or live their lives. This is going to be a very hard day for everyone. The families talk about how the girls loved the outdoors and exploring around. The girls were joined at the hip and always together, doing something.

"It's the worst feeling in the world to know your daughter is out there and you can't do anything to help," Rhonda says.

"When they didn't come back and we couldn't reach them, we feared the worst," Kay says in response, through tears.

They tell me they reported the girls missing after they hadn't heard from them. The police filed a report but never got any leads. This went on for years and years until the case went cold.

"We never gave up hope. We knew someday the girls would be found. We got our prayers answered the day we got the call. We knew there wasn't much hope the girls would be found alive after all this time and we are just grateful to be able to give the girls a burial and lye them to rest" says Rhonda.

We talk about things the girls loved to do and the places they loved to visit. The families were so proud of the two girls. They had so much to live for and so many dreams to accomplish. It is sad that it was all taken away from them.

It is time to take them to where the girls were found. The ground is dry and not so muddy anymore. I lead the way ahead of them talking about the trees I planted for the girls. We get to the spot and I stop, pointing out where the girls were located. We hold hands with lots of tears flowing. We pray together and cry together.

"Is it ok to lay some personal items down in the area they were found?" Kay asks.

"Absolutely! you can leave whatever you like," I tell her.

We go to the trees I planted and the two moms tie a ribbon of the girl's favorite color on each of the trees.

"We can't thank you enough for finding our girls" says Rhonda.

"I am glad you now have closure and can give them a final resting place" I respond.

"My husband never gave up hope. It destroyed him and he passed away 2 years ago. I think he died of a broken heart" Kay sobs.

"He was never the same after we lost her. My wish was to find her before we both passed, but at least now she can be buried next to her dad," she continues.

We make it back to the deck where we sit and talk some more. They are so happy they made the trip and so thankful for the discovery.

"Would it be ok if we come back every year for the anniversary of the day they were found?" Rhonda asks as she hugs me.

"You can come back anytime!" I answer.

She then asks if she can quickly go back to the site by herself, to take some pictures of the area and the trees, so she can show family members. Kay and I hang back on the deck sitting in silence and drinking coffee.

It is time for them to leave and head back home. They gather all their stuff and get ready to go. We hug and say our goodbyes, with tears flowing from all of us. *It isn't goodbye, it is more like until we meet again,* I think to myself.

Over the years it will be interesting to see how big the trees I planted will grow. I will forever remember this day and how much these girls meant to their families.

THE WEATHER IS STARTING to get colder and I am getting low on firewood, so I grab some to bring inside. It's nice living in the woods, where the trees can be cut down and used for heating all winter. I sit and wonder about all the animals out there and how they survive the cold.

Well, it's been a very long day, so its time to settle in for the night. I have an exciting day planned for tomorrow. I love going on all my adventures. I watch some tv and head to bed around midnight.

It was a good sleep and now it's time to get up and get ready for the day. With a coffee in my hand, I head out on to the deck. I love the sound of the birds and the smell of the fresh air. The planes overhead and the traffic on the road can be heard in the distance. Now to enjoy the next hour or so contemplating my day. *Where to go and what to do? Do I walk or do I drive this time?* I'm thinking I will drive and take a few off roads. I finish my coffee and head inside to get ready. After packing the cooler, I head to my car.

I make my way down the highway and try to find a road I have not been on, but that's hard as I think I have been on most of these off roads. I head to the right as I see an open area and a tan color car sitting here. Now this got me thinking. *How long this car has been sitting here? Does someone own it or is it stolen?* Now to park and get out for a closer look. I don't see anyone around the area. There are no plates on the car. As I look inside, I see some papers that look like bills and junk. I can't make out a name on the paper. There are no keys and the doors are all closed, but they are unlocked. I slowly open the door to get a closer look. Nothing out of the ordinary, other than papers and garbage in the car. This is when I notice a few shell casings on the ground. *Could there be a body in the trunk?* I think to myself. I don't see any blood or evidence of a struggle. I am so eager to get the trunk open, but I don't want to pry it open. There is no smell coming from anywhere, so I decide just to leave and come back in a few days to see if it is still here.

I leave and decide to make my way down another dirt road leading off of this one. I drive around and find a few more dirt roads to explore. As I get closer, I can see another parked car. Its not uncommon to see parked cars in these wooded areas. I think, *maybe someone is just taking a walk through the woods.* It could be someone hunting or fishing. I drive up to it to see if I can get a closer look. I get up to the window and can see 2 people inside. I bang on the window, but they don't move or respond to me. I walk to the other side to get a closer look. They are still not moving. I begin to panic and think, *are they dead or sleeping?* I don't want to open the door in case I startle them, but I am scared something has happened to them.

I call the police, give them the location and tell them the people are not moving and I think they are dead. After about half an hour, the police arrive. They open the door and realize I have just discovered 2 dead bodies.

I am shocked and wondering, *what happened to them?* One of the police officers takes me aside and asks me a ton of questions.

"What are you doing in this area and how did you come across the car?" he asks.

"I was out exploring around, as I do quite often and came across the car," I respond.

The officer takes my name and info down, then says he will contact me in a few days. I immediately leave and go a bit farther to another dirt road. I stop a few times and take some pictures. I love taking pictures of old farmhouses and shacks. I drive around for a few more hours before deciding to head home. It is getting late and chilly, so it's time to get back to the cabin.

It takes me over an hour to get home. I am tired and hungry. I can't wait to get my shoes off and relax. I grab my cooler and water bottle to bring inside the cabin.

I make supper and decide to sit on the deck to watch the stars, while thinking about my day. I realize after sitting that I'm actually not very hungry, so I only eat half of my chicken sandwich and some cucumbers on the side. I go inside at about 9pm and get ready for bed. Once I'm in my pajamas, I watch the news for less than an hour. It's 10 o'clock and I'm wiped. It has been a long, adventurous day and I need sleep.

The next morning, I get a call from the police. "The 2 bodies you found in the car had committed suicide. We found a suicide note, but still have to perform an autopsy to determine the actual cause of death" says the officer. I thank him for calling and let him know that I am glad I could help. I guess I was just in the right place, at the right time.

I CAN'T WAIT TO get dressed and adventure out again, to see what today brings. I decide to make an apple pie and start a pot of chicken stew for when I get back home from adventuring. After a few hours of cooking, it is time to get ready and head out once again. I get dressed and pack the cooler.

Today, I decide to go for a long drive to find a hiking trail a few miles away. I love the smell of the outdoors and hiking through the woods. I pull into the parking lot and it is packed with cars. I get a parking spot close to the road, then grab my backpack and water bottle, before heading to the trail.

I see a few people who have dogs along the way. I continue walking the trail and see a spot overlooking some rocks. I make my way to the open area to look down below. I can see trees and lots of bushes. I am thinking, *can I find a way down there to explore?* All of a sudden, I can hear someone down below but can't see anything. I need to get closer. It sounds like two people screaming at each other. I try to listen and find out where the noise is coming from. I look down over the ledge to see a male and female having a very loud argument, but I can't hear what they are yelling about. I wait and listen for a bit longer. The arguing gets louder and louder. I can sense something is wrong and she seems very upset.

She is screaming "PLEASE DON'T HURT ME, JUST LET ME GO!"

I hear the male say in a loud voice "WE ARE DONE!" and he pulls out a gun.

I watch in horror as he shoots the female in the head. She falls to the ground limp and he immediately drags her body by her feet. He puts her behind some trees and I am trying to take notice of what he looks like. I need to call the police and tell them everything, but first, I have to wait and see what happens next......I wait patiently.

I am in total shock and just want to go down and try to help her but I know it is too late. She was shot in the head and I saw her body hit the ground. After a few minutes, I can see him making his way to the trail. He keeps looking around, but there is nobody else here except me. I hide, so he doesn't see me. Quietly, I follow him down the trail and out to the parking lot where the cars are. I am hoping he has a vehicle so I can get a description for the police.

I can't believe I just witnessed a murder. *Why didn't he just let her go? Why did he have to shoot her in the head?* I say to myself. We get close to the parking lot and I stay hidden, but watch him get in his truck. I need to get closer to get a plate and the make of the vehicle he is driving.

I take a picture of what he is driving and get a plate number for the police. I know the area and the trail, as I have hiked it several times over the years. He leaves after about 5 minutes, so I call the police from my car and tell them what I just witnessed, then ask them to come take a look. They say it will take them about 45 minutes, but they are on their way and will meet me in the parking lot.

I wait patiently, which seems like forever for them to get here. After 50 minutes, the police finally arrive. I go over to their car as 2 officers get out and I tell them I am the person who called. I take them through the trail where I witnessed the shooting of the woman. As we get to the top, I point down to the area where they were standing. I tell them what tree he dragged her behind, so they can find her.

They make their way down to the area and walk behind the tree. I see the police officer come out from behind the tree and make a phone call. I can hear him talking about a female body that is in a wooded area. One of thc officers comes up to where I am, to get all the information on the suspect in question. I give them the description and the make and model of the vehicle, along with the plate number. They ask me if I can describe what he was wearing and how tall he was. "He is wearing jeans, a dark grey hoodie, about 5' 10" wearing a black baseball cap" I say.

They are sending someone to try to locate the individual and take him in for questioning. They tell me I can leave, but will probably have to point him out in a line up later on. I agree and make my way to my car to head home. It has been a very busy and stressful day. That poor girl. *Why would someone shoot and kill someone? Why not just go your separate ways and each one move on?* I think. Her life is over and now he will spend his life in jail for this. Life is so precious and can be taken away in a split second.

I TAKE MY TIME driving back home. It is a beautiful day, but didn't turn out the way I wanted it to. I am glad to be home. I grab my cooler and other items, then head inside.

I am hungry so I sit, eat supper and think about how lucky I was today and how it could have gone in a different direction if I was seen by the man. *Would he have shot me too if he saw me witness the shooting?* I think worriedly. I am so glad I got out of there without being noticed. I sit for a few hours on the deck after supper, taking in all the sounds of the animals and how peaceful it is here at the cabin. I go inside around 9pm and get ready for bed, but watch a bit of tv before finally going to bed around 11pm.

It is a very restless night. I wake a few times, but stay in bed until 6am. I get up and make coffee, before going out on the deck. This is my happy place. It is very quiet and peaceful. I sit for about an hour and then start to plan my day. *Where will my adventures take me today?* I wonder.

I go inside to get a few things done before leaving. At about 9am, I get a call from the police who tell me they have a suspect in custody and want me to come identify him in a line up.

"Are you able to come in today at 11 to identify him?" asks the officer.

"Yes, I can be there for 11" I say.

"Okay, we will see you then" he says before hanging up.

I get dressed and head to the station. The traffic is heavy, so I am trying not to be late. I get to the station just before 11am and the officer meets me at the door to explain the process. He takes me to the line up where nobody can see me, but I can see them. I immediately point him out as the man I saw shoot and kill the woman.

"Are you sure that is the man you saw commit the murder and shoot the woman in the head?" asks the officer.

"Yes, I am sure. That is him" I say.

"That's all we need" he responds with relief.

They get me to sign a few papers, before letting me leave. I can't help but think how this guy took a life and now he will spend the rest of his life behind bars. It just doesn't make sense to me. *Why not just walk away and move on?* It's a question I keep asking myself.

I LEAVE THE STATION and head home to pack, then head out again on another adventure. There is so much to see and experience in a lifetime. I love exploring and seeing what everyday has in store for me.

I decide to head to the highway and take another look at the abandoned car I'd seen a few days before. When I get to the road, I turn in. The car is still here but this time it has a smashed door and window. It looks like someone drove into it with another vehicle. They pushed the door in and the window is shattered. There is glass everywhere. I think *maybe it was someone out for a joy ride and saw an abandoned car, so they trashed it.* I leave and drive further down the highway.

I would love to find an old farmhouse and explore the inside of it. There are not too many around that aren't on private property, so I will have to be careful not to trespass. It's amazing the things you can find, that people just leave and forget about. I drive up and down several roads, taking in all the sites. I see a few vehicles in passing, but it is getting late, so I decide to head home. I put the music on and listen to some good old country songs.

As I make my way home, I can't help but notice all the animals along the way. I see so many cows, horses, deer and even moose along the way. I pull over to the side of the road and take a few pictures. The nice thing about living in the country, is that the scenery and animals are so beautiful. I make my way back on the highway and it takes me about an hour before getting back to the cabin.

I am tired and need some food. I go inside, get some supper ready, eat, then go outside on the deck. I look through my phone at all the pictures I took today. I delete some and keep a few I like. Now, to plan tomorrow's adventure. I am thinking of going to town, having breakfast and going from there. I watch some tv and decide at midnight to call it a night. I need to get some sleep. I make sure the door is locked and go to sleep.

At 6am, I wake up and make my way to the deck with a hot coffee. It is still a bit dark, but relaxing at the same time. I can hear some animals in the distance. I sit relaxing and after an hour, go inside to get ready, so I can head to town for breakfast. I leave my house at about 9am because I like to get there a little later, when the traffic is not so heavy and people are already gone to work.

I am trying to decide between 2 different restaurants. I end up picking the one that makes the best poached eggs. I like my eggs a certain way and this restaurant makes them the exact way I like them. I arrive at the restaurant and it looks busy.

I go inside the restaurant and sit by myself, at a table for two. There are a lot of people inside having coffee and talking. The waitress comes over and takes my order, which is very simple. She brought the coffee pot with her, so I give her my cup and order two medium poached eggs with 1 slice of light rye toast. No butter. Suddenly, I can hear what sounds like 2 men talking in the booth behind me. I can hear them talking about killing one of the guys wives. It sounds like one of the guys hired the other guy to kill his wife.

"Man, I can't take this anymore, I just need her gone" says one of the men.

"Are you going to do it or not?"

"Yes, I can do it" the other man responds.

I think, *can this really be happening?* I listen closely, trying to look, but not to be seen. I can't make out everything they are saying, because they are talking quietly; however, what I do hear is disturbing...

"I will be gone that evening so it's the best night to get the job done. I will pay you $5000 up front and the other amount when I get confirmation that you have fulfilled your duties. Not a minute before," he says.

"Consider it done. Soon, we will both get what we want. New life, new dreams," the other man answers.

My food comes and I am trying to eat quickly, in case they get up to leave. I want to follow them. The waitress comes to their table and asks if they need anything. "Just the bill" says one of them. They get the bill and head to the till. One of them pays and they both go outside. I get up from the table and put cash on it, to cover the bill and a tip. I didn't even finish my delicious breakfast, but at least I managed to eat one egg and my toast.

I go outside, where I see the 2 of them talking by a black truck. After they are done talking, one of the guys leaves and walks over to another vehicle. Now I know I need to follow one of them, but which one is the question. They both have separate vehicles. I decide I will follow the guy that has the black truck. I get in my car and wait for them to leave. I follow the guy with the black truck for about 15 minutes, until he turns off on a dirt road. I know going to the police that this will be considered hearsay, without any "real" proof. For all I know they could be writing a book or doing a movie script.

I drive slowly and carefully behind the truck until he turns into a driveway. The house is big and has a barn on the property. At the end of the driveway are 2 big red wagon wheels and a large wooden mailbox. I see a few horses and dogs on the property. I decide to leave now that I know where one of them lives. Taking a chance, I drive away thinking, *maybe they will be meeting tomorrow at the same place.* I decide that I will go back in the morning and check.

I decide to head back to the cabin to get some chores done, that I have been putting off for so long. It takes me about 20 minutes to get home. The traffic is light and I don't see any animals this morning. I can't help but wonder, *what if, this is really happening? What if, someone is really planning a murder?*

I STAY OUTSIDE FOR most of the day getting things done and spend some time by the trees I planted for the 2 girls. They are growing a little more every day. I stack some wood and pick up some garden hoses, then start a fire in the outdoor fire pit, to burn some brush and old wood. The yard needs a real good cleaning. I rake a little and throw everything in the fire pit to burn. Finally, I head inside to make some supper. Sitting by the firepit to eat, I watch the fire for a couple of hours as it burns down to ash. The sky is beautiful.

It's getting late and I am tired. I head in to watch some tv and do my dishes, before putting my pajamas on. I shut the tv off, lock the door and go to bed. I toss and turn all night and don't get any sleep.

Finally, I get up at 5am and go on the deck with my coffee. The birds are out and I can see a few planes flying up above. I can only dream of being on a plane right now headed to a deserted beach. I go inside to do my dishes and get ready to go to town. I want to get to the restaurant early and get a seat in case they show up. I don't want them to see me come in and leave when they leave.

I arrive at the restaurant for 8am and sit at the same table as I did the day before. She pours me a coffee and I order a piece of toast. I decide not to get poached eggs again. After about 10 minutes, I notice the restaurant is starting to fill up quickly. There are only two tables left. One right next to me and one on the other side of the restaurant. I worry if they do show, they will decide to leave or sit too far from me. Just as my toast arrives, the men do as well. They make their way towards the empty table beside me and sit down.

Now I can hear everything and need to find out if they are actually planning a murder. The men order just coffee.

"Tonight's the night you need to get this done. Be at my house for 10pm. I won't be home and she will be alone. You need to make it look like a robbery. Shoot her and trash the place, then take some jewelry and get the hell out. Fast!" the husband says.

"Okay, are you sure there will be nobody else in the house? I can get the job done, but I don't want to get caught and end up in jail," the other guy answers.

"I'm sure," he says.

I know they will be leaving soon, so I need to get out of the restaurant before them and wait in my car. I pay my bill and wait, listening to country music and watching for them to come out.

The 2 guys come out and are talking for about 5 minutes. They both get in their vehicles and I decide to follow the other guy today. The house is very small and rundown with boards on the windows. I am thinking this guy seems like he is really hard up for money. It sure looks like he is struggling and that's the reason he agreed to do this in the first place. I leave and decide to go to the police.

I GET TO THE police station and ask to speak with an officer.

"Just have a seat and someone will be here to help you in a few minutes" says the lady at the desk.

"Thank you," I say as I sit down.

A few minutes later an Officer comes out and introduces himself.

"Hi, I am Officer Ken, how can I help you?" he asks with a smile.

"Well, my name is Jill and I have some information regarding a possible murder about to happen" I say.

"Oh!" He says surprised.

"Well, let's go talk in my office."

I follow Ken down the hall to an office on the right-hand side.

"Come in. Please take a seat and tell me about this possible murder," he says.

"Well, I was having breakfast at a restaurant and I overheard 2 men talking about killing one of their wives. It sounded like one guy was paying the other guy to kill his wife. I followed one of the guys to see where he lived. I wrote down the plate number and the address. The next day they met again at the same restaurant. I followed the other guy and got his address. It looks like the husband is well off and the other guy might be doing it for the money," I say.

"Well, when do you think this is supposed to be happening?" asks the Officer.

"It is supposed to be happening tonight," I answer.

"Thank you for coming in. Please write all of your information on this paper and we will investigate this further" says the Officer as he hands me a paper.

"Thank you and I hope you can save a life tonight" I say.

I finish writing my contact info down and he stands to shake my hand, as I walk out. Well, this isn't good enough for me. I decide I must go tonight and make sure the police go there. I'm not about to let a murder take place.

I leave the station and go for a long drive to clear my mind. I can't help but think, *why wouldn't you just leave or get a divorce? Was it for the money or life insurance? Who would be that cruel to plan their own wife's murder?* I hope the police take this serious enough to check it out. I head home to get some supper and things done before I go out tonight.

It's about 7pm and I'm getting ready to go to the house and see if this is really going to happen. I leave my cabin, head out to the farmhouse area and park on the road a bit farther down. I walk through the woods where I can still see the house and find a large rock to sit on. Thankfully, no one can see me. A few minutes later the police arrive in 2 unmarked cars. I see 2 police officers exit the cars on the passenger side and go up the driveway to knock on the door. A lady answers the door and I can see them talking to her. She lets both officers inside the house and a few minutes later the drivers leave, heading down the road.

It's getting late and I'm starting to think the guy supposed to kill the other guy's wife has changed his mind. It's also starting to get cold and I'm tired. Finally, at 11:15pm, I see a car pull up and park on the road. It's the guy from the restaurant that lives in the boarded-up house. I think, *why he is showing up over an hour late?* I now know he is going to go through with it, but he will get the surprise of his life when he enters the house. He gets out of his vehicle and sneaks up the driveway with what looks like a large gun. He is dressed in a black hoodie and is wearing jeans. I see him at the door and he is trying to unlock it. It seems like he is struggling to get the door open. He finally gets the door unlocked and heads inside. Within a few minutes, I can see the police escort him out of the house in handcuffs and place him in the back of a patrol car. There is another police officer pulling up. He gets out and goes inside the house.

I am hoping the police can track down the woman's husband and arrest him. She must have been so scared when the police told her why they were at her house. I know I would have been.

I decide to head home before they see me. I drive slowly and can see another police car pass me. I think, *are they going to the house also?* I make it back to the cabin and I am so thankful nobody got hurt tonight. Hopefully, these guys will spend their life behind bars.

I make a coffee and sit on the deck until almost midnight then head in to try and get some sleep, after this eventful day. I go to bed and can't help but think about what has just happened. I am going to call the police station in the morning to thank them for trusting me and saving this woman's life.

I have a restless sleep and wake up still tired, at about 6am. I get up and head out on my deck with my coffee, then at 8am decide to call. I ask to speak with Officer Ken.

"This is Jill" I say.

"Oh, hi Jill!" Officer Ken responds.

"I was just calling to ask if you responded to the report I made and if anything ended up happening?" I ask.

"Ah, yes. Last night was a success. We were able to arrest the guy when he showed up and the husband of the woman was found and arrested, shortly after. Both men have been charged and are awaiting a court date," he informs me.

"Will I need to testify if there is a trial?" I ask nervously.

"No. Thankfully, both have admitted to the crime and are willing to plead guilty. The husband was having an affair and instead of telling his wife, he decided to have her killed. He contemplated doing it himself, but he could not pull the trigger. We are very thankful for the information you gave. You should be very proud of yourself Jill, because you saved a woman's life," he answers.

"I guess now he thinks he should have just told her and walked away instead of spending his life behind bars," I tell him.

We say our goodbyes and end the call. I don't need to testify, so I decide I have to go talk to the woman at the farmhouse to make sure she is okay and tell her who I am. I decide to get ready and head over to her house around noon. When I arrive at her house, I see are a couple of cars parked. I knock at the door and a woman answers. "Hi, I am Jill and am wondering if I can speak to the woman of the house" I say. She invites me inside, to where there are about 5 other people in the living room. I introduce myself and tell her what I heard and how I wasn't about to let a murder happen.

"Oh, I am so glad you were there. The police officer last night came to my door and told me what was about to happen. I was in complete shock about what my husband had planned. You were very brave to take matters into your own hands. My family and I are so grateful for your decision to step up and stop this from happening." she tells me.

"I am just glad you are okay," I respond.

"We have been married almost 7 years and couldn't have kids. My husband wanted kids, so that could be why he was having an affair. We talked about adoption, but my husband wanted no part of it," she sobs.

"I am so sorry to hear that. I am going to go and let you spend your time with your family. If you're okay with it, I would like to leave you my number and you can feel free to call me anytime you want to talk," I tell her. I don't want to overstay my welcome.

"Oh, that would be great! Thank you so much," she answers.

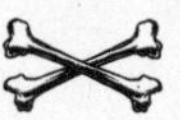

I SAY GOODBYE TO everyone and head to my car. This doesn't make any sense. If you love someone, there are other options out there. As I am walking down the driveway, I find a wallet. I open it up and it has a health car inside with a name and medical information, a debit card, and a folded-up piece of paper with a name and address on it. The address is of the farmhouse I am at right now. I think, *could this have belonged to the guy that was hired to kill this woman? Did he drop it as he made his way up to the door last night?* I keep it and decide to drive to the police station and hand the wallet in. I tell the lady at the front desk where I found it and about the situation last night. This wallet might be important to the case, so I leave it with her and she says she will look through the cases from last night and give it to the appropriate officers. She asks for my name and thanks me for my help.

I GO FOR A drive, pick up some groceries and head home. I think to myself, *I really need to take a vacation.* I decide to start looking online to see where I can go relax for a week. I find a nice resort in Mexico and think, *this is just what I need.* I look through all the pictures to make sure there is a beach and a swimming pool. The resort looks amazing, so I book it and I leave in a day. I have been to Mexico a few times and love it there.

I am excited about lying in the sun for a week. A week will go by so fast, but it's better than nothing. I bring in some bins from the shed that have some summer clothes in them, then I pack a suitcase and get other personal stuff ready. It takes me an hour to find my passport, but I find it.

I decide to on a nice long walk, down the road since my packing is now all finished. I think to myself, *maybe a little adventure in Mexico will be nice.* I just want to get away from everything, relax and just enjoy myself.

I get home and make sure I have everything I need, since I am leaving to go to the airport in the morning. I pack very light and just take what I need for a week of laying in the sun, on the beach. I realize I forgot to back my suntan oil and finally find it under the bathroom sink in a large baggie. It smells like coconut. I also find some after-sun lotion in case I get a burn. I go over my check list to make sure I didn't forget anything. I am so excited. I don't think I will get any sleep, but I must try. I can always sleep on the plane if need be.

I head to bed and wake in time to finish last minute things before I head to the airport, like throwing out food that will go bad and making sure all the windows are locked up. I take one last look in my suitcase to make sure I have everything I need, then call my family to let them know I am leaving. This way, I know they will check on my place while I'm gone. I get to the airport and check in. There are so many people at the airport. I hear them call for my flight going to Mexico and get in the line to board the plane. I am so excited for this trip.

I booked my ticket for a first-class seat, so I get to board first and have lots of leg room. I get on the plane and put my carry on up above my seat. I get comfortable and take my shoes off, then wait for the plane to head down the runway. It isn't long before I can hear, "please fasten your seatbelts and stay seated." Up, up and away we go.

After we get up in the air, the flight attendant comes around with a hot cloth and asks if I would like a drink. I think, *well I'm on vacation so why not?* I order a drink and a snack, then get comfortable in my seat. I know the flight is going to be at least 8 hours. I can't stop thinking about laying on the beach in the sun, but I have to remember to be careful the first few days. I don't use tanning beds, so I will burn very easily.

After many hours on the plane, I arrive in Mexico. We have to wait until the seatbelt sign is turned off before we can get up. Finally, after a few minutes the seatbelt light goes out and everyone starts getting up from their seats. I stand up to get my carry-on bag from the compartment above my seat, while the door opens. We start climbing down the stairs one by one. I am the 4th one off because I flew in first-class. There is no better feeling than arriving and having the heat hit you as you walk off the plane. We all have to grab our luggage and find our bus to the resort we are staying at. It is so hot and I can't wait to check in and hit the beach. I have shorts on under my pants, so I take my pants off, roll them up and put them in my carry-on bag. I take off my thin jacket as well and shoved it in my bag.

The bus ride is over an hour, but they have coolers full of beer for a buck. Ice cold beer on a hot day? This is my kind of vacation! You can hear everyone talking and a few people start to sing. The bus driver speaks up and says "we are almost here, so please get your things together." We come to a stop at the front doors of the resort and hand the driver a tip as we step off the bus. I am known to forget the tip at times and thankful others got off first, so that I am reminded. I guess it's all the excitement of travelling.

I make my way to the front desk where it is starting to get busy. I just want to check in and get my room key, then head to the beach. The line up takes over an hour to get through. I am finally at the desk and give them my name. They have everything ready and say "enjoy your stay!"

I make my way to the elevator and to my room. I check out the view from my patio deck and can see the beach. There is also a very large swimming pool and a swim-up bar. I am in heaven. I quickly change and make my way to the beach, grabbing a drink along the way. There are so many people here. I grab a towel from a large storage shelf and find a nice lounge chair to lay in. I put on some sunscreen and relax, then try several different fruity drinks. They go down fast. It is hot and I am enjoying every minute. I realize how late it is getting, I am also pretty hungry. I don't want to leave, but I know I have to eat. I decide to go to my room and get changed, before heading to the restaurant for some great food. I am hoping to have some shrimp and lots of pineapple. I get on the elevator and go down to the restaurant where I can smell the food. I can see so many cooks and so much food. This is something I enjoy when I travel, the great food and the fantastic beaches.

I get in line and grab enough food to keep me full until tomorrow. There are so many different things to choose from, but I get my shrimp and pineapple. The good thing about an all-inclusive vacation is you can eat as much as you want and go back for more.

I sit alone and enjoy my meal, then get up to grab a drink and dessert. The place was busy when I first arrived, but is clearing out fast. There are just a few people left sitting down. I sit close to a couple who look like they are very much in love. It makes me happy to see people in love and looking very content together. They are holding hands and I can hear them talk about how it must be taken care of soon. I wonder to myself, *what must be taken care of soon*? I try not to eavesdrop, but sometimes it's hard not to. I keep listening and what I am hearing is very disturbing. It sounds like they are plotting to murder his wife. My back is to their table, so we can't see each other. From what I can hear, the man is married and having an affair with the lady he is sitting with. I can hear them talk about how they are planning the murder and when they are planning to do it. They are getting ready to leave so I decide to follow them. I need to find out if this is really happening.

They head down to the floor below mine, holding hands and giggling. As the man stops at room 17 to scan his key card, I walk past with my head down and they don't even notice me. I keep walking trying to figure out what to do next. As I'm walking, I hear noise coming from down the hall. I look up to see a beautiful game room. The walls are glass and I can see people on the left sitting at tables doing puzzles and board games. Others, stand on the right playing pool and throwing darts. There is also a bar on the far wall. I head inside, grab a strawberry daiquiri, and sit at a table facing the hallway. I don't want to start playing anything because I won't have time to clean it up when I leave. I can't see the door to their room, so I can only hope that when they leave, they decide to walk this way.

Thirty minutes go by and I see the man dressed in a uniform walk past. I leave my empty glass in a tray by the door and follow him. He walks all the way to the front desk where he walks behind the counter. I realize now he works here at the resort. I ask another worker if there are any police I can talk to. They want to know why, so I briefly say it's private and I have info on a possible crime about to happen. They agree to help me and call the police to meet me at my room.

I go up to my room and wait about an hour before two police officers knock on my door. I invite them in and begin telling them my name and that my visit to Mexico is just for a holiday. I continue talking to them about what I overheard. They say this is a serious crime, if it's real. I give them the room number and tell them he works at the front desk. They say they will take it from here and will be in touch.

The next day, as I am waiting to hear from the police, I decide to scout out the room they are staying in. I make myself blend in so I won't be noticed. I walk past the front desk and can see the man behind it. Now to head to the game room and wait to see if the lady comes out. She walks past and as I go to follow her, just like I had followed him, I see two people enter the room she just left. I stand beside the game room entrance looking at the plants beside on either side of the door. After about 5 minutes, the two men come out and begin walking towards me. I notice as they pass, that they are carrying badges on their belts. Slightly hidden by suit jackets. *They must have been undercover police officers* I think to myself.

I go back downstairs to the lobby and decide to head to the beach and see if she is there. She is lying on the beach alone. I decide to go sit close to her and see if she will talk to me. I order a drink and she does too, then I introduce myself.

"Hi, I am Jill" I say.

"Hi! I am Wanda" she replies.

We chat like we have known each other for years. She is very young and pretty. “I have been coming to Mexico for the past 7 years” she tells me. She comes to the same resort for a month at a time and hopes to move here some day. We talk about where I am from and have a few more drinks. We realize it is getting late and we haven’t eaten anything all day. We both need food. She asks me to join her at a table to eat, and maybe head back to the beach afterwards. Well of course I agree. We put on beach cover up and go to find a seat. You are not allowed to enter the restaurant in a bathing suit. We eat and talk for over an hour before heading back in the sun.

“I love coming to this resort. This is my favorite” she tells me.

“I haven’t been to this resort before” I respond.

“It is amazing and the staff are so friendly” Wanda says.

A couple hours later, she says she has to go meet someone and that she might see me the next day at the beach. I say goodbye and stay at the beach for another hour before going to my room. I get ready and head to the lobby to see if there are any police around, so I can ask them if they found anything. I want to make sure they are taking me seriously about this possible murder. I sit and have a drink. Finally, I see the officer I had spoken to originally. I approach him and he takes me aside. “We have everything under control” says the officer. He thanks me for my help. I’m not quite sure what he means, but I take it as they are still here, so they must be investigating it.

I want to enjoy the rest of my time in Mexico, so decide I did what I could, now it’s up to the authorities to take over. I don’t have much time left. I want to enjoy the little time I have here before I get back on the plane to head home.

The next day I don’t see the lady anywhere or the guy from the front desk. I am approached by an officer who thanks me for what I told them.

"We have arrested both with the planning of a murder. We were able to plant cameras in the room they were staying in. We were given access to his room from management because he works here. We got them planning the murder on video and they will both be doing jail time" he tells me.

"Well, that's great news" I say.

Just a few days left before I head home, so I want to get as much sun as I can before I get back on the plane. I think to myself, *why didn't I book 2 weeks instead of 1 week?* I spend my remaining days at the beach and my evenings listening to the entertainment at night. It has been a great holiday and I am so happy I saved a life. I get to enjoy the rest of my last few days, before I get ready to leave.

The day has come to pack up my suitcase and head to the airport. I wish I could stay forever, but I can't. I check out and wait for the bus to take me to the airport to board the plane back home. The bus arrives and it is time to go. An hour later, we arrive at the airport. I grab my luggage and make my way inside to check in. I get my boarding pass but I still have to wait another 3 hours before I can board the plane.

I walk around the airport and decide to sit and have some lunch. I find a place to eat and wait for them to seat me. I order fish and chips and an ice-cold beer. The restaurant is packed full of people. I am glad I got a seat. I am tired but wish I could have been able to stay longer. I get my beer and after about 10 minutes my food comes. I don't have to rush so I take my time and enjoy every minute of my vacation. I finish my meal and wander through the airport to see if I can find a souvenir to bring back home. I come to a little store that has some sweatshirts with Mexico on them. I decide to go in and buy a nice navy blue one. I don't like hoods, so I find a sweater without one. It is time to make my way back to my gate. My flight is boarding in 30 minutes, so I grab a seat until they call first class up to board.

It is time to make my way through the gate and head onto the plane. I get on and settle in for my flight home. After everyone boards the plane, they tell us to fasten our seatbelts and stay seated until the seatbelt sign is turned off. I must have fallen asleep because I wake up to the sound of "we will be landing in 30 minutes." I think to myself, *did I sleep that long?* I must have slept over 5 hours. I had to have been tired. The flight attendant comes by to ask me to put my seat up in the up-right position. After about 30 minutes we are on the ground. We land safely. I had a wonderful time.

NOW, IT IS BACK to reality and heading home to my cabin. I get inside the airport and wait for my luggage to come through. After about 10 minutes the luggage starts coming. I watch for mine and quickly grab my one and only suitcase. I know it is mine because I tied a bright red ribbon on the straps before I left home. I get my bag and head outside to grab a cab. I have to share a cab with someone going in the same direction as me. At this point I really don't care who is in the cab. The cab driver drops the other person off and we continue to my cabin in the woods.

After giving him directions to my cabin, we finally make it to my driveway. He drives up to my step and gets out to help me with my luggage. I thank him and pay the fee.

I had somewhat of a relaxing holiday but also got an adventure in as well. I can't wait to tell my family and friends about my trip. They will be shocked to find out about the planned murder I solved. I guess I was in the right place at the right time, once again.

I keep telling myself *maybe I should have been a detective.* I love exploring around and going on adventures to see what I can find. I never thought I would find a body, witness a murder or stop a murder.

I love to watch crime shows and read true crime books. I also love to be outside, exploring around different areas and taking off-roads. When I see a new road, I always wonder, *what I will find down here?*

I get settled in back home and unpack my suitcase. I throw a load of laundry in the washer and put the suitcase back in the shed, then I call my family and tell them I am home safe and sound. I make snack and sit down to plan tomorrow. Well, I know it will include venturing out and seeing where I land. The washer stops, so I put the clothes in the dryer. I make a coffee and sit on the deck until my clothes are done. I fold the clothes so they won't wrinkle and decide to head to bed shortly after midnight. I need to try and get some sleep.

I TOSS AND TURN all night, before finally getting up at 6am to the chirping of birds. The day is starting out great, as I sit out on the deck with my coffee. I am glad to be home and excited to go on a hiking trip.

I come inside and decide to pack some food in the cooler, so I can venture out. My drive is about an hour away, so I want to get on the road early. I am going to hit up a trail containing some waterfalls. Leaving at 8am, I crank the tunes and drive for almost an hour. I get to the trail leading to the waterfalls and grab my backpack, before heading down the trail. There were a few cars and people around in the parking lot. I just go on my way, by myself. I walk for about 20 minutes, until I come to where the waterfalls are. I make my way down the steep bank and can see so many people hanging out. There are people on the beach and some by the falls. I also see people walking in the water, which is very shallow. I take a few pictures and enjoy the scenery. The air smells so fresh and there is laughter all around. *This is my kind of day*, I think. I decide to stay a little longer and relax in the sand. I am watching the people in the shallow water. Some of them are fishing.

Suddenly, I hear a lady scream! People start running over to see what is going on. I decide to go get a closer look. When I get here,

I can see that someone hooked a sneaker with their fishing line. As I take a closer look, I can see what looks like a foot inside the sneaker. I think, *what in the world is this? Is there a body in the water?*

"I will call the police!" I yell.

"Everyone should get out of the water until the police arrive!" I yell again.

There are a lot of people who are leaving with their kids, but I want to stay and see what else they will find. About an hour and a half later, the police arrive to get a closer look. Without a doubt, that is someone's foot. The police tell everyone they need the names of everyone here and then we all need to leave. We give the police our info and leave.

Well, I don't leave. I decide to go along the trail up high so I can overlook what is going on. I find a rock pile that I can hang out at until I know more about what is happening.

I wait about a half hour and can see the police pull up what looks like clothes. They find a hat and a backpack. Within an hour, the place is full of police and divers. I know it will be very hard to dive there in the shallow waters. The police put a large tarp down on the ground and everything they find is placed on it. There are a lot of items and what looks like parts of a body. Within a few hours, the tarp is filled with items and body parts. The police continue to rope off the entire area and call in more people to help.

It is getting dark, but I can still see people coming and going for hours. There are people bringing food and setting up tents. *Is this going to be an all-night thing?* I think, to myself. I decide to head home and get out of the woods, since I can't see where I am going in the dark. It takes me about 35 minutes to get out of the woods. I don't want to fall and I don't want to get caught by the police. It's hard enough to walk this trail when its daylight and I know it will be a struggle at dark. I don't want to use the flashlight on my phone in case the police see the light. I take my time and when I can finally see my car, I stop in the woods and wait for a few minutes, sipping a bottle of water. I want to make sure there is nobody around when I leave, I still have to drive almost an hour to get home.

I drive on the dark highway and don't see much traffic. I think, *what a day it has been.* I just want to go back and see what else they will find in the water.

I get home but know I won't get any sleep. I just keep thinking, *who could that have been and what happened? Was it a drowning or maybe a murder?* I make a coffee and sit outside on the deck until at least midnight, letting my mind wander. I am already planning to head back there in the morning. I decide I am going to sneak up to the rocks where I won't be seen again. I know it will be a very long day but I have to go back and watch. I head inside to try and settle in for the night. I know the police are all set up and are going to be there all night. I might have stayed if I was better prepared but it would be a long cold night alone on the rock with no supplies. I can't wait to get up and go again. I shut the tv off, lock the door and climb into bed. I toss and turn, before finally getting up again at 5am. There is no way I am going to be able to sleep.

I make a coffee and head outside on the deck. I am so pumped to get on the road and go back. I finish my coffee and get ready to go with my backpack. I can't eat any breakfast right now, so I make a couple of sandwiches and some snacks. I grab a few bottles of water and pack everything in the large backpack I have. I don't take the cooler because I won't be able to carry it all up the hill, to the rock. I put everything in the car and go back to lock the door. It is a beautiful day, but I need to remember to grab my light jacket in the back seat, in case it gets chilly. I'm not sure how long I will be there. I want to be prepared just in case I am there until night fall.

I head out at about 7am. I have to go through town to get gas first then back track the other way. I grab a coffee after I get gas and head out on the highway. I can't help but think the same thing again. *Who was that in the water and how long were they in there for?*

What happened to them? I need to know. I put the music on for my drive to try and distract my thoughts.

I finally arrive and see so many police cars. The parking lot is blocked and they are turning everyone around. I see a few cars being told to leave and I am asked to leave also. I go down the road and make my way back to where I know I can get through the woods without being seen. I park my car and walk a bit to make it through the woods and up the hill. There is a spot in behind the outhouse to climb up and take cover. I know I won't be seen here. The police are so busy monitoring the parking lot, that I am able to slip through without being noticed. I take my fully packed backpack with water and food, along with my jacket and head up the trail to the rock pile. I know there is so much going on that nobody will notice me. At least, I hope they won't notice me.

I make my way to the rock pile and I get settled. I know I will be here for a while, probably close to dark. I can see so much spread out on the large blue tarps now. There are police everywhere and divers in the water patrolling with what looks like large hooks. They are still pulling stuff up and placing it on the tarps. After a few hours of watching, I can see they are getting together in a group and talking, but I can't hear anything. It looks like they are done and going to take everything they found to be analyzed. I can see them with bags and bags of items. They start carrying everything up, I assume to load into their vehicles. I see a white van parked and think, *is that the coroner's vehicle?*

I'm not here as long as I thought I would be. I only have enough time to eat one of my chicken sandwiches and a cinnamon bun, before they are done packing up. I pack up my items and grab my water bottle to get ready to go down the bank without being seen. I know I have to leave soon. I wait a few minutes to make sure they are done.

I decide to make my way back to my car before I am seen. I head down the trail and can hear people talking. It seems like they are very close to me. I wait and look around to make sure I don't bump into anyone along the way. I sit for a little while until I think it is safe to head down in the direction of my car. As I get closer to heading down the steep hill, I can see police everywhere. I freeze and have to wait a little longer until it is safe to keep going without getting caught. I can see that they are still asking people to leave the area. I don't want to get caught passing them, but I have to go this way to get to the outhouse. I am hoping there will be nobody in the outhouse, or they might ask what I am doing here. I finally get down safe and can head to my car undetected. There are still police everywhere and cars driving close to mine to turn around. I manage to get to my car and wait a few minutes before leaving. I want to head home and watch the news for updates on their findings. I have to take my time today though, because there is so much traffic on the highway. There are a few cars pulled over on the side of the road and everyone is going so slow. It looks like someone has hit a deer. The little cute red car is not so cute anymore. The front end is smashed but it looks like the driver is out of the car and unharmed. There are a couple of vehicles that stopped to help, so I just continue on my way home.

I ARRIVE AT MY cabin and take my backpack inside. I empty my food out and put everything away. I still have a sandwich left so I eat it for supper, then I put the news on. It doesn't say anything about the body in the water. I make a coffee and relax on the deck for an hour or so. It is a beautiful evening for sitting out here. The later news is starting soon, so I head inside to watch it. I wonder if this one will say something about the body. Sadly, there is nothing mentioned.

One week later...

Finally, a sketch is released of the person found. They are looking for anyone with any information on the identification of the person in this sketch. I watch the news for months and months after, but they never release a name. After so long, there is no more mention of the body and the sketch never hits the news again. *Is this going to be another unsolved case?* I wonder.

THE WEATHER HERE IS getting colder everyday but it's so peaceful out here in the woods. It's time to prepare for the colder days as summer is coming to an end. The evenings sitting on my deck are getting shorter and darker. I wrap up in a blanket and watch the stars. If you are lucky, you will see the northern lights. They are so beautiful and colorful.

The leaves are starting to fall off the trees and fill the yard. The wind blows and the leaves gather in piles. It is amazing to watch. I love to take drives in the fall when the leaves are this colorful. The animals are also getting ready for the cold winter that is ahead of us. I don't walk as much in the cold but I still like to go on adventures while driving.

Halloween is not that far away. I remember going out as a kid and getting so many treats. I like to see all the kids dressed up in their costumes. I live in the woods, so I don't get any kids out here but I enjoy going to town and watching all the kids in their costumes. The scarier, the better.

I decide to make candy apples this year to hand out in town to my friend's kids. It is a busy day but I get them all made. I'm bringing 18 to town tomorrow. I make some red ones and some caramel.

I decide to dress up this year and deliver the apples to my friend's kids. It is a long day making these apples, but they are worth it. I clean up the mess and make supper. It is getting late and time to relax out on the deck. I watch the dark sky and it looks like snow is not far behind. I head inside around 11 and try to get some sleep.

At 6am, I wake up and feel refreshed for the day. As I make my coffee and head outside on the deck, I notice it is snowing very lightly. I am hoping it isn't too cold or slippery tonight when I head to town.

I spend the day cleaning and wrapping up each apple to bring in. I put a small fire on and relax for a few hours. It is getting late, so I decide to get ready to head to town. The kids go out around 5 o'clock, so I want to make it into town on time. I leave my house at 4:00 and arrive in town around 4:30. The roads are snow covered but it is very mild out. I deliver all the candy apples and watch the kids go house to house collecting treats. The costumes are amazing. It sure brings me back to when I was a kid. I think about all the houses I went to and all the treats I would get. The heavy pillowcases so full I could barley lift them. By the time I would get home my pillowcase would be so dirty at the bottom from dragging it, that my mom would throw it in the wash before going through our treats. Good times and beautiful memories.

Well, it is getting late and the streets are bare, so I decide to make my way home as the light snow hits the streets. I don't think it is too slippery out but I don't want to take any chances.

THE TRAFFIC IS GOING very slow, due to the slippery roads. I take my time, as do the other vehicles. I notice the car in front of me swerving back and forth. I stay back so we won't hit each other. Suddenly, the car loses control, hits the guardrail and rolls down the bank. I slow down and finally come to a stop. I get out and can see the car flipped upside down in the water. There are no other cars to flag down for help. I go to my car and grab my phone to call for help. I give them directions and tell them they will see my car, along with the description of it, so they will know where I am. I head down to see if I can help in any way, and can hear someone screaming and trying to get out.

The car is sinking, and I can't do anything. I feel so helpless.

I can see someone climbing out the driver's side window. I yell to let them know I am here to help. I can see the person swimming towards me. It is dark but I keep yelling to come this way.

"I see you. Keep following my voice. I am here to help you" I scream.

Finally, he reaches me. He is cold and wet. I ask him if there is anyone else in the car.

"No, just me "he says in his shivering voice.

"Stay here. I called for help, and I am going to my car to get a blanket for you, and we can wait together," I tell him.

I run up the bank and grab a blanket from my backseat. I make my way back down to him and realize he is nowhere in sight. I yell and yell thinking maybe he is hurt and wandered off in the woods. I yell some more and finally I can see flashlights coming over the bank. It is a couple of police officers.

"I'm down here" I yell.

The officers make their way down the bank to where I am standing. I begin to tell the police "There was a guy that got out of the car and swam to me. I ran up to my car to get him a blanket but when I got back down, he was gone." We search but have no luck finding him.

"I didn't get a good look because it is so dark and everything happened so fast. I did ask him if there was anyone else in the car though and he said no" I tell the officer.

"Well, we need to get search and rescue here just in case he is hurt and needs medical attention" the officer tells me.

The police take my name and my info and tell me they will contact me if they need anything. They say they will be getting someone to come get the car out of the water but that won't be until tomorrow, when they can see clearer.

It is time to head home and get warm. There is nothing else I can do but wait and see if this person is found. I hope he doesn't have to spend the night in the woods. It is freezing rain and getting colder by the minute.

I make it back home safe and sound. I shovel off my step and then go inside to run the bath water. I am cold and wet and need to get warm before I get sick. I put a fire on while my bath water is running. I pour some bubble bath in my water before getting in. It feels so good to get warmed up. I make a hot chocolate and sit by the fire. I can't help but think about where that poor guy is. *Is he cold or lost? Did he fall or is he hurt?* So much goes through my mind and I pray he is found alive and well. I turn on the tv but there is nothing on the news, other than the roads are slippery and to drive with care. There is nothing about the accident on the news. I watch a few shows before going to bed.

I wake a few times through the night and don't get much sleep at all. Finally, I get out of bed at 6am to start my day. I get the fire on, before making a pot of coffee. I go out on the deck for about 10 minutes and come back inside to sit by the fire. I am still chilled from the night before and can't stay out there. I keep wondering if the guy has been found. The roads look good and most of the snow has melted. I guess it isn't cold enough yet for it to last. I decide to have some toast with peanut butter and my coffee. I need to go back to where the car is in the water. I need to find out if they found the guy who climbed out of the car.

I DECIDE TO GET dressed and go back to where the accident was. I start my car and let it warm up for a few minutes while I finish getting ready. I head out around 11am to the scene of the accident. As I approach the site, there are cop cars along the side of the road. I park my car and try to make my way down to where everyone is. I can see them trying to get the car out of the water. As I make my way down, I am stopped by a police officer.

"You need to go back up and leave" he says.

I tell him who I am and that I am the one who reported the accident the night before. He is glad to see me and says they need to talk to me, to get some more information about the accident. A couple of officers take me aside and ask me questions to try and get a better description of the guy. I am not much help with that, because it was so dark.

"He has a small face tattoo on left side below his eye. It looked like a tear drop. He was so cold and wet I just wanted to help, so I went to grab a blanket for him. When I got back with the blanket he was gone. I yelled in case he was hurt and was roaming around in the dark but he didn't answer. I wasn't gone too long, so he couldn't have gotten too far," I tell him.

"Did he give you his name or tell you anything at all?" He asks me.

"Nothing," I respond.

Finally, the car is up and they are calling in the license plate to see who the vehicle is registered to and maybe that will help them ID the guy that is missing. They look inside the car and are shocked at what they find.

There is a deceased guy strapped in the passenger's side. They ask me about this and I tell them that I was told by the other guy, there was nobody else in the car. The one guy climbed out the driver's side window and the car sank.

The car comes back as stolen. Now everything is starting to make sense about why the guy lied and why he ran off. They search the trunk and find bags of money and a couple of guns.

Upon further investigation, they realize there were 2 robberies yesterday. These guys must have stolen the car and robbed a couple of places. They were on the run until the accident happened. The police ask me to go downtown to look at mug shots in case I can ID the guy that ran off.

I decide to follow one of the officers to the station. As I arrive, he takes me in a room to look at mug shots. It is so hard to tell, but I manage to find 2 people that it could be. The police leave and when they come back, they tell me that 1 of the guys is still in jail and the other guy was released 3 weeks ago.

Now they have somewhere to start. They also get an ID on the body in the car. It turns out it was a friend who did time with the guy who ran and they were both released the same day. Looks like they were up to their old tricks again. They certainly didn't waste anytime getting in trouble again. Now, the hunt is on for this guy and to bring him in for questioning. They know he will be hiding out somewhere. They need to try to track down any friends or family he might have in the area. They even check the local hospitals to see if someone fitting his description might have checked in.

They tell me he has a sister in the area and they will see if he has made any contact with her. It appears he doesn't have any other family and has had a hard life growing up. They want to get on this right away so nobody else gets hurt.

The officer tells me I am very lucky and this could have turned out very differently for me. This guy could have made me take him in my car or hurt me in some way. I guess I am very lucky with the way it turned out.

Four weeks later...

I get a call from the lead investigator of the case. He tells me they found the guy and he will be charged. The officer tells me the guy had contact with his sister and they staked out her house until the arrest was made, then he thanks me for all my help.

I am glad it is over and nobody else got hurt. This could have gone a million different ways if he hadn't been caught.

IT IS A BEAUTIFUL Sunday morning when I decide to ask my neighbor Hope and my friend Bella to go on an adventure with me. They both say they would love to come explore with me. I tell them to pack a few things and meet me at my house around noon. They both arrive and we finish getting the cooler and my backpack ready. We like to pack food and drinks, when we go out for the day. We pack my car and head out on an adventure.

We head down the highway and find a trail to take. We drive for about half an hour listening to music and being silly. We are trying to decide what road to take. We take a road that we have never taken before. We park the car a few minutes later and get out. We stand there taking in the fresh air and grab our stuff to head down a trail. We had been walking for about twenty-five minutes when we stopped to take a few pictures. You can see we are up high and love to take in the scenery. We take a few pictures of ourselves as we always do. We love to spend time together and talk about all the adventures we do together. It is so peaceful up here and the view is amazing. I can spend all day looking at the beautiful colors of nature surrounding us. We spend about 20 minutes overlooking the area and take a few more pictures, then I notice something sticking up from down below. It is hard to make out what it is.

We are so far up and looking down it seems so small. White fragments lay in pieces below. We decide to head down the bank to get a closer look. We need to take our time and pretty much slide down most of the way. There is no way to get a car down here. As we get closer, we could tell it is part of a plane. It looks like a wing and has some writing on it. We get closer and realize it is indeed a plane. There are parts all over the place. It looks to be a smaller plane. As we get closer, we are in shock to see 2 people strapped in their seats.

There is blood everywhere and we know there is no chance at all they are alive. Now to try to get some help and call the police to inform them of what we found.

Bella decides to climb back up the bank and call for help as we have no service down below. Hope and I look around and find parts all over the place. I can't believe the plane didn't explode. It looks like it had clipped a few trees and hit hard coming down. We find some luggage in the area and try to get something with a name on it but have no luck trying to figure out who these people are. They are just filled with clothes. I am wondering how long they have been here. I haven't heard anything on the news about a missing plane.

Bella makes her way back down to where we are. Looking at me with a grin, she says "the police are on their way and we can't touch anything." "Ya, like that's gonna happen" I say. Hope says "we just need to be careful and they won't know". We find 4 more bags that we hope will contain personal information. I open one of the bags to see if I can identify who these people were.

I am in shock to find the bags are full of drugs. All 4 bags have drugs in them. We decide to lay the bags by the plane and let the police handle it. I guess this was a drug deal or shipment that was being delivered somewhere.

After about an hour and a half, we can hear the police up above. We yell and wave for them to see us down here. A couple officers head down the bank where we are. They can't believe we have found a plane. They take a closer look and can see the 2 bodies inside the plane.

We show them the bags and are asked a few questions. They take our names and information. I ask the police if there was any news about a plane lost or missing people. "No, not that we are aware of right now, but we will investigate it further" says the officer. This is not just a lost plane. This was a drug dealer doing deliveries and probably isn't a registered plane.

"We have all your information and you girls can leave now" said one of the officers. "We will be in touch if we need to ask anymore questions." They call for more authorities to come help and figure this out. They need to get the bodies out of here and try to find out who they were.

All 3 of us make our way back up the bank. I take a bunch of pictures before we climb up the steep bank to the car and it is a lot harder than it was going down. What a day this turned out to be. What an adventure. We get to the car and wait for a few more police and the coroner to show up. They take body bags and stretchers down to retrieve the men.

We watch from the car for awhile, until we can see the bodies being removed from the plane. They put them into the large black bags and onto the stretchers. We watch as the officers struggle to get the first body up the steep bank. All of a sudden, one of the officers trips and lets go of the stretcher causing all of them to tumble down to the bottom. It all happened so fast with no time for them to react.

We hear screaming and jump out of the car to get a better view. People are scrambling towards the bag looking distraught and frantically trying to move the body bag. I take a closer look and notice something sticking out from under it.

"The body is on top of the police officer" I say in a panicked voice.

"I hope they aren't hurt," Bella says.

"Well, we know the dead guy isn't" Hope chuckles.

We continue watching as they all get up unharmed. After taking a few minutes to compose themselves, they successfully get the bodies up the bank. We don't want to be stuck behind them so we decide it's best to leave now, while we still can.

The 3 of us talk all the way home about our adventurous day. This was a day to remember. Hope and Bella ask me when our next adventure will be. I quickly tell them any day they want to go. I am a phone call away and always ready. We arrive back at the cabin. Hope and Bella drop me off, then head home.

I make some supper and sit to watch the news. They talk about the discovery of a plane that was found in the woods. They give a location and hope that someone will come forward. They say the plane was discovered by a few girls taking a hike in the area. Our names were not given but it sure felt good to know it was us that found the plane. I can't wait to go back to the area and see if the plane is still there.

I WAIT A FEW days and decide I have to go back. I call Hope and Bella to come with me and they both tell me I shouldn't go back there. I have to go back and check it out. I want to snoop around in case the police missed anything.

I have supper and start to plan my day for tomorrow. I know I have to be careful. I need to get a good night sleep and make sure to take the camera. I want to take lots of pictures.

I sit out on the deck and have a coffee. It is so peaceful and a full moon is out. I just love to sit outside before going to bed. I stay on the deck for about an hour before heading back in the cabin. My legs are still sore from climbing a few days ago, so I need to rest.

As I get ready to go to bed, Bella calls and says her and Hope want to come with me when I go back. I am happy they have changed their mind. I tell them I will be leaving at 10am tomorrow morning. We all need to get some sleep. I head to bed at midnight and I am so pumped about tomorrow. I can't wait to wake up, pack and go.

I get up at 7am, make coffee and head to the deck. I sit on the deck for over an hour listening to the bird's chirp. It is so peaceful here. I decide it is time to start getting ready. I go inside and get dressed, then wait for the girls to show up. I pack the backpack with food and water. I didn't eat any breakfast and know I will get hungry along the way. I make some chicken sandwiches and take a bag of Oreos. I finish getting dressed so I am ready when the girls get here.

At about 9:30, both Hope and Bella show up at the cabin. They talk about how we must be careful and maybe we shouldn't go. I tell them we will be fine. We are just going to look around. It is going to be exciting. I am just wondering if there is anything left behind that the police might have missed.

We head out and talk all the way about the plane. What are we going to find that the police might have missed? We finally arrive at the spot where we had to climb down the bank to the plane. We can see the plane is roped off with yellow tape all over the area. But it is still there and that's all we wanted. We make our way down to the plane. The steep bank seems so high up. As we make our way to the bottom, Hope gets her pants snagged on a branch that is sticking out. We laugh at her expressions and continue laughing all the way to the bottom. I am just glad I get to the bottom without getting hurt.

We spend an hour looking around, taking pictures. We can see stuff the police left here. I can't help but wonder why they left so much stuff at the crash. I would think it would be important to take everything to solve the case. We find water bottles and a backpack full of food. We also find a map. These are things that can be important to the police to solve this case. We can't figure out why and how they missed this. *Why was it left behind?* I wonder. We just take pictures but leave everything. We think maybe the police will come back and finish looking around.

I am getting hungry, so are Hope and Bella. They are always hungry. We sit to the side and have a sandwich and some Oreo cookies. We always pack food and drinks. Hope brought some veggies and Bella brought cinnamon rolls. We have lots of food to enjoy. We enjoy our time together and try as much as we can to explore and go on adventures.

We can hear what sounds like people talking up above. We decide we should go behind a few trees and wait to see who it is. We can see people looking down to where the plane is. We are well hidden. After a few minutes we see a couple of men coming down the bank to get to the plane. We need to stay hidden because we don't want to get in trouble for being here. One of the men is over 6 feet tall with a long beard and the other guy is short. They are both wearing hoodies and both have hats on. They are also carrying backpacks. The make there way down the bank until they reach the plane.

They are looking inside and around the area. We hear them talk about how they must find the bags. We know they must be looking for the bags of drugs the plane was carrying. They say over and over they must find these bags, or they will be killed. It sounds like the 2 men know the other 2 that died in the plane. We are so scared they will find us. We stay hidden and very quiet. I think we are all thinking the same thing. *If they find us, what will happen? Will they kill us? Will they think we found the drugs?* They keep searching the area, but they have no luck finding the bags of drugs. I take a few pictures of the guys discreetly. They know the police have already been here. They stay for a few more minutes and say the police must have found the bags. They decide they better leave before someone shows up. The 2 of them make there way up to the top of the bank.

We wait to make sure they make it back to the top and we can hear them leaving. That was a close call. We know we have to leave. We climb back up to the top and make it to the car. I am contemplating on going to the police with the pictures. I don't want to have to answer as to why I came back here. I decide to just leave well enough alone and not give the police the pictures. I know it will somehow work out. We drive around for a few more hours to enjoy the rest of the beautiful day. We explore a few more dirt roads and take some pictures of the scenery, along with some cows.

We head back and get to the highway. I can't help but wonder if the plane is going to stay there or if they'll try to get it up in pieces. I think they have everything they need and the main concern is to find out who these 2 people found in the plane were. At least the drugs were confiscated and won't hit the streets.

We talk all the way home. This could have gone so wrong if those men had found us snooping around the plane. We are glad we got out of there safely. This is an adventure we won't forget. We had another exciting day together.

We make it back to the cabin and sit on the deck to talk over an hour. We look through the pictures I took and now I wish I would have taken the map. I don't know why but it would have been nice to save it.

Hope says "we should get together and plan another adventure soon."

"Ya, anytime. Say the word and I'm in. Don't have to twist my rubber arm" I say.

Bella laughs as they walk out the door and head home for the night. Time to make supper.

It is a beautiful evening. I sit on the deck after supper until about 9pm and then go inside to get ready for bed. *Let's plan my next adventure,* I think to myself. I am going to venture out tomorrow to see where my little car takes me. *What direction should I try tomorrow?* I think to myself. I watch a few shows I have taped before shutting the tv down for the night.

I have a good night sleep and wake at 7am. I make a coffee and go out on the deck. The weather is warm and the trees are colorful. It is peaceful sitting all alone. As I look up, I can see a moose in my yard just behind my little shed. I try to capture a few pictures, but it is well hidden. I can only get the front of it. I have gotten pictures of moose and deer in my yard many of times.

My phone rings at about 10am. It is the police calling to say they have names for the 2 people found in the plane. They don't give me the names but want me to know the families were notified. I ask them about the recovery of the plane and am told it will remain where it is. There is no way they are going to tackle trying to get that plane up the steep bank. It is basically in pieces and would just be falling apart. They say they have everything they need with the plane and will not be going back to it.

The police inform me that one of the sister's wants to thank me for finding her brother. I am glad I helped and they now have closure.

I COME INSIDE AND decide it is time to venture out again and explore some trails or dirt roads. I am not sure what I am going to do, other than pack the cooler and get in my car. I get dressed, sweep my floor and put a chicken stew in the slow cooker. In order for it to be done at the right time I put it on low. *Don't forget to grab some water and make a sandwich for the road,* I think to myself.

I leave about noon to wherever I land. There isn't much traffic on the road, but it is slow driving. There are a few large trucks holding up traffic. I drive until I see an area that might be interesting. I want to get off the road because it seems like it is taking me forever to get anywhere. I never know where I will end up, so I am usually prepared just in case I get lost. I drive up and down a few roads before I find one to take. This road looks like it had traffic on it recently. I take that one and drive about half a kilometre when I notice what looks like a big steel barrel. It looks old and dirty and has fire ashes all around it. It is off to the side at the edge of the woods. I stop and get out to get a closer look. I see inside what looks like burnt clothes and other items I can't make out. It sure looks like someone left in a hurry. Some of the items are not totally burnt. Maybe they started the fire and thought it would burn down to ashes. Whoever did this, needed to get out of here fast. They didn't wait for the fire to finish burning. I can't help but wonder what or who they were burning. I know I want to find out what is in this barrel. It is too heavy to try to move, so I must try to I push the barrel over. I just need to see what they were trying to burn.

I try to tip it upside down, but it is a little too heavy. I continue to kick and kick it until it finally falls on its side. I roll it and some of the stuff is coming out. As the stuff is coming out, I try to roll it more to get it to empty out. It gets lighter so I am able to tip it upside down and get it all dumped out on the ground. There is so much that didn't get burnt. I find clothes and at the bottom is a purse and a watch. They are scorched but you can tell what they are. There are no signs of a body, but I know this doesn't make sense out in the middle of nowhere. *Who would come to an isolated area and burn someone's personal items and why?* I can't help but think *this is defiantly a crime area but where is the person this stuff belonged to. Was it just a bad break up or did something happen to someone?* I am thinking *I should call the police but now I just disturbed all the evidence.*

I wait a few minutes and think I better call just in case there is someone in trouble or missing. Maybe they can get something off the purse or watch I found in the barrel. I call and tell the police what I have found. They are coming to take a look for themselves.

I wait about a half hour for them to show up. They arrive on scene and take a closer look. "It looks like something weird happened here. Why did you tip the barrel over and dump everything on the ground?" asks the officer. "I was curious and didn't think nothing of it at the time" I tell him.

The 2 officer's bag all the items they can find so they can get it to a lab for a closer look. They walk around a little bit to see if there is any trace of anything else in the area or close by. They find a cell phone that looks like it was tossed in the woods. Now this really got their attention to thinking this could be a crime scene. They try turning the phone on, but it is cracked and possibly dead. They bag it to take in for evidence. I walk through the woods to try to help find anything I can to help them. They tell me if I come across anything not to touch it because it has to be bagged. I walk a bit further where I find a ladies white Nike sneaker. There is only one so I continue deeper into the woods and discover the other one a few feet away. It looks like they were tossed here. I yell to the officers, and they come to bag them both. Now is the time they ask me to go by my car and stay there. I am not sure if any of the stuff we found has anything to do with the burnt items in the barrel.

I can hear them say "I got something." One of the officers is heading my way. He tells me they found a shallow grave, covered with dirt and leaves but are unsure what is buried in it. As they start to dig the shallow grave, they find a human leg. They now have a crime scene. The officers continue to dig and come across a few body parts. One of the officers steps away and is as white as a ghost.

"Whoever is buried here, is buried in pieces," he says.

"Someone dismembered the body. We need to rope the entire area off and get the forensic team in here," says one of the officers. As they dig and dig, they come across pieces of a female body. A few feet from this grave, is another shallow grave. One of the officers starts to dig. "I have a leg over here!" he yells. I think to myself, *whoever is responsible for this crime, took their time to hide the body. They must have spent hours here digging holes to bury the pieces. They will need to find out if the actual murder happened here or if this was the drop off. Did they kill her somewhere else and bring her here to bury her?*

"Did you see anyone in the area or any vehicles while you were here" asks the officer.

"No. The traffic was slow, so I got off the highway and took a few dirt roads to explore, as I often do." I respond.

"Well, I will need your name and personal information, then I need to ask you to leave. I will be in touch with more information as it comes." He tells me.

As I try to leave the area, other officers pull in blocking the exit. They brought shovels and go to where the other 2 officers are. They rope off the area with yellow tape. I can see them taking pictures of tire tracks and the barrel with the other items that were found.

Another officer asks who I am and what am I doing in that area. I tell him I was out for a drive when I came across the barrel and tipped it over. He asks me if I saw anyone in the area and for my name. I tell him the other officer has all my information. He signals for the officer blocking the exit to move and I agree to leave the area to let them do their jobs. I know I will return the next day to see what they found, or didn't find.

I leave and head down another dirt road. I drive about 15 minutes, then turn around. I can't help but think about the body that was buried. *Who was she? Why would someone do this?* I know she wasn't there very long because the fire in the barrel looked like it had happed recently.

All the way home I can't help but think about that poor girl. *Did she suffer? Did she have family or kids? Who could have done this and why?*

I get home and go inside the cabin to check on my chicken stew that I can smell as I get out of my car. I change into some comfy clothes and put on the news. I am wondering if there will be anything on the news about the body found. I dish up some stew and sit down. As I am eating my supper, the news shows the area I was in today.

It shows there was a body of a female found today in a shallow grave in the woods. "There will be an on-going investigation to try to find out who did this" the news reporter says. There is no name released as they are still trying to find out the identification of the body. "Anyone with any information about a missing young woman around the age of 25-30 should contact their local police department."

I am glad to have taken that road today or maybe she would never have been found. I guess I was in the right place at the right time. I finish supper and make a coffee, then go out on the deck. The sky is still bright and it is very peaceful listening to the animals in the distance.

I go inside around 8pm, clean up from supper and do my dishes. I watch some shows and head to bed early. Tomorrow I am going to head back to the same place the body was found. I just want to look around the area and see if there was anything they missed.

Getting up at 6am, I make myself a coffee. I need to grab a sweater before hitting the deck, because it a little cool out. I grab my nice fleece sweater that my dad used to own. *This always keeps me warm and he is forever with me,* I think.

I can hear the traffic going up and down the highway. It seems like a very busy kind of day today. I drink my coffee and go inside about an hour later. It is still early so I decide to make another coffee and toast with peanut butter. I had a restless night and can't help but think about that poor girl buried in a shallow grave.

I finish eating, get dressed and then get ready to go look at the area again. I make a third coffee to take with me in my to-go mug. I just want to make sure they didn't miss anything that could help them solve this crime.

I head out around 10am. The traffic isn't as heavy as it was yesterday. I have to try to remember the road I took. When you are driving on dirt roads sometimes, they all look the same. I make it to the turn where I know I went, but now must find the road I went down. There are so many that look the same. I drive down one and realize it isn't the right one. I turn around and try another one. I know I have the right one this time because I see a cop car coming toward me. I just keep driving and listening to music until I get to the spot. There is nobody here, but I can see yellow tape through the bushes.

I park my car and make my way through the woods. It isn't very long before I can see the shallow grave. I look around but don't find anything close by. I walk around some more and find a sock. It is red but very dirty. I'm not sure if it belonged to the victim or not but think it might. I carefully pick it up with a stick and place it near the shallow grave in case the police come back. They will see it and take it in to be analyzed with the other items.

I spend an hour or so just walking around the area and going deeper into the woods, but don't find anything else. The barrel is still here but they have it standing upright. I look inside but it is empty. There is still ash all around the area. I decide it is time to leave and head in another direction. I take a few different roads and finally make my way to the highway to head back home. It is only 4 o'clock but it has been a few long days. I need to get home and put a fire on. I am getting hungry and want some left-over stew I made yesterday.

I make it back to the cabin and go inside to have supper. I sit down with my stew and a piece of bread and butter. After a nice supper, it is time for a coffee and to sit on the deck. I end up staying on the deck for a few hours. I call a few friends and chat about old times. I was going to call it an early night and try to get some sleep but that doesn't happen. It is almost 10pm when I finally go inside and I am already planning an adventure for tomorrow. I do my dishes and watch tv for a bit. There isn't much on, so I head to bed. It has been a long day.

I WAKE AT 7AM, after having a nice long sleep. I feel refreshed and ready for the day. I have my coffee out on the deck and decide I want to go walk along the water today and find some trinkets or beach glass. The weather is getting cold so I'm not sure how it will be by the water. But I decide to take the chance and go walk the beach.

I get ready and head out around 10am. I have the cooler packed and jump in the car to head down the highway. I am looking forward to a long day by myself.

I get to the road where I want to walk down the trail to get to the beach. I park my car and see an old gate that is locked. There are no signs anywhere, so I go through the gate and make my way to the water. I have heard it was a nice beach to go to. It isn't that far of a walk, but it is downhill and through the woods. I make it all the way to the water. I walk and walk along the shore until I come to what looks like a little shed close to the woods. It looks small, but new. I am thinking I am on private property, but I don't remember seeing any no tress passing signs along the way. So, I go up to the shed to take a closer look. It is locked. I think, *why there would be a shed here in the middle of nowhere unless this is someone's property?* I can't see inside so I walk around the shed. I go around the back of the shed and there is a window up high. I decide to go look for something to stand on so I can take a peek inside. I drag over a few pieces of wood and stack them up, then I climb up and can see through the one and only window.

As I glance around the inside of the shed, I can see a large board hung on the wall with pictures and paperwork. I really need to get inside and get a closer look. But the door is locked and I don't want to break in. I can see pictures of people and some news paper clippings hanging on the board. It is hard to make out the faces or names on the newspaper clippings.

I wait for a bit and decide I should just leave. I start to walk towards my car when I see a couple of people coming towards me. They are talking and I don't think they see me, so I head towards the woods to hide out see where they are headed. I am still close to the shed, so I go in behind that area. They head to the shed and unlock the door. I make my way down a little closer to see if I can hear them or see inside. They go in and shut the door. I climb up to the window and look inside. I need to be very quiet, so they don't see or hear me. They are talking and I can see them take down the pictures and all the news paper clippings. They put everything in a bag and say they need to burn it all. After about thirty minutes, they start towards the door. I get down from the window and lean against the back of the shed.

I can hear them talk about family and how they got what they deserved. They talk about their parents and how other family members took advantage of them. This apparently was a family feud and these two guys took matters in their own hands, taking care of a few family members who stole everything from their parents. They didn't say what they did other than the problem was solved. I'm not sure what they did or if they did anything at all. I have no proof, but they did say their parents didn't deserve what the other family members did to them. I hear them say that both parents were not alive anymore and they waited a long time for this day. They both leave and start heading towards the way they came. I wait until I know they are gone and not coming back to the shed.

I come out from behind the shed and go to the door, but they have locked it. I want to get inside to see if they missed anything or dropped any pictures. I think, *maybe I should come back tomorrow and see if I can pick the lock*, but I know that would be wrong. I can't go to the police because I don't have any evidence of anything and it is all hearsay. I leave and head back to my car.

As I climb back up the hill to my car, I can see the 2 guys sitting in their truck. I know it is them because of the hats they are wearing. I just play dumb and go to my car. I don't think they even saw me, or at least I am hoping they didn't. I don't want them to stop me and ask me where I was. I just want to get in my car and get the heck out of here. I think, *that was a close call. What if they come back? What were they doing sitting here all this time?* I'm not sticking around to find out. I leave and never look back.

I hit the highway and can't wait to get home. I want to go online and see if I can find anything about members of the same family getting murdered. I drive about ten kilometers when all of a sudden, I hear a popping noise and my car starts shifting all over the road. I have blown a tire. I am alone and on the side of the road with a flat tire. I have never changed a tire before in my life. I don't want to be here in the dark. It is going to be dark in about an hour and I need help.

I have no cell service so I can't call anyone. I am just hoping someone will see me and stop to help. I wait and put my hood up so a car will see me if they drive by. They will see I am having car trouble and hopefully stop to help. After about 15 minutes, there is a truck coming towards me. I am relieved, when they stop to offer help. As they get out, I can see it is the 2 guys from the shed. They ask me what if I am okay.

"I blew a tire and have a spare, but don't know how to change it." I tell them.

"We can change your tire for you" one of the guys says.

"Thank you, so much." I tell them both.

I open the trunk and the guy grabs the spare. They change the tire within a few minutes and tell me to drive safe. They are 2 very nice well-dressed guys. They don't say anything about seeing me earlier so maybe they didn't notice me. I thank them and drive off. My heart is pounding thinking about how much of a close call that was.

I make it home safe and sound. I go in to make supper and know I must head to town in the morning to get a new tire put on. I want to keep my spare in the trunk in case this happens again.

I eat supper and then go on the deck with a hot chocolate. It is a beautiful night and so many stars are in the sky. I head inside at about 9pm and get ready for bed. I watch some tv before shutting it off around midnight. I keep thinking, *I should go back to the shed and see if there is anything left behind*. Curiosity is killing me. I decide that after I get a new tire in the morning I will head back and break the lock. I just need to get inside that shed. I know I shouldn't, but I will try not to damage anything other then the lock.

I have a good night sleep and wake at 7am. I make a coffee sit in my usual spot on the deck. It is a beautiful day and I watch as a couple moose walk through my yard. It is time to go inside. I need to get my new tire from town and head back to the shed. I get ready and grab a pair of lock cutters along with some snacks, then I throw everything in my car and head to town. I am not sure if I even have the strength to cut the lock, but I am going to give it a try.

I get to town and need to wait an hour for the service guy to put a new tire on for me. He puts my spare tire back in my trunk and off I go. I need my coffee so I go through Tim Horton's drive through and get a coffee along with a donut. I am about an hour away from the beach and hoping there is nobody around. I don't want to get caught busting in a shed that isn't mine.

I get to the gate at about noon and decide to head down to the beach. There is nobody in the parking lot. I grab my backpack with the cutters inside in case someone is on the beach. I don't want them to see me with the cutters. It is a bit of a walk to get to the shed. I walk close to the woods in case there is someone around. I make it to the shed and don't see anyone. Quickly, I take out my cutters and try so hard to cut the lock, but I don't have the strength. I have to pound and pound the lock until it finally breaks, then I open the door and go inside. *It sure is creepy*, I think. I know I shouldn't be here, and I am trespassing. My heart is pounding, and I start to look around. I don't find any pictures, but I do find a book. I open the book and can see what looks like names and a schedule. It is a brief description of the family and what has happened. I want to read it all, but I don't want to get caught. As far as I can see, there is nothing left in the shed to look at so I decide its best to leave. I put the book and cutters in the backpack. I decide to read the book at home. If those guys come back, I will be in trouble.

I just want to get out of here, but I need to try and figure out how I am going to get the lock back on because it is now broken. I guess I should have thought about that before I broke into this shed. Well, I can't really be concerned now. Maybe they will think it was a bunch of kids looking around.

I walk back to the parking lot, jump in my car quickly and lock the door. My heart is racing. I didn't see anyone around, but I am still nervous. Now it's time for me to get out of here. It is only early, so I decide to take another road and see what else I can find.

I drive for about 20 minutes when I spot another dirt road. I don't think I have been down this road before, so I just have to go look. I drive for a few minutes, when I finally see an old, abandoned farmhouse. Well, at least I think it is abandoned. I have always wanted to go inside and look around an old farmhouse. I must remember this place because its so easy to forget what roads I take.

All that is on my mind at this time, is to get home and read the book I found in the shed. I am hoping it will solve some unanswered questions about the pictures and newspaper clippings. There isn't much traffic on my way home. I listen to music and have my window cracked a little to get some fresh air. I arrive home as it is just starting to get dark, then go inside with my backpack in my hand. I am so hungry; I need to make some supper. I want to make a quick simple supper, so I don't take too much time cooking. I want to eat and sit quietly so I can get into reading this book. I am hoping for answers.

I put a small fire on and take this time to sit and relax. I grab my sandwich that is cut in half. I get the book out of the backpack and start reading. I start to understand so much about these 2 guys I saw at the shed. They wrote so much detail in the book and it is starting to make sense. It goes into details about how a family member took advantage of his elderly parents. It states how he convinced them into signing their house over to him and they could live there until they passed. It states that both parents showed signs of dementia, so they were taken advantage of. The oldest brother had a home of his own and he would pay the estate a very low amount of money when he sells his house. He never tried to sell his house because he had no intentions of paying for his parents house.

The book says that another family member found all this out and went to their parents. The parents said they signed everything to the oldest because he took them to a lawyer and had it done. They were never given a copy of any paperwork of the documents. This raised red flags for the 2 brothers. When they approached the oldest brother, he knew he was caught. Apparently, the whole family ended up finding out. The oldest brother talked to a few of the siblings who agreed to back him. He told them they could take whatever they wanted out of the house, including paying off one of the siblings with their parent's money. This made the family split up into different directions as everyone had a different opinion of the whole situation. The 2 went on the say they weren't going to let him get away with it. The book states that both parents are now deceased, and the oldest brother sold his house and moved into the parent's house. The brothers were so hurt that the oldest got the house for free. He ended up not paying the estate any money because the parents passed before he sold his house.

The book goes on to say the family is torn apart but nothing in the book says what happened to the family members. I guess they didn't want to write anything down in case they got caught. The ending in the book says the family got what they deserved and now the rest of the siblings can move on. The siblings that agreed with the oldest brother about what he was doing must realize now how wrong they were.

Wow, this sure is an interesting read and I can really relate to this story. Life is so short and this just goes to show how greedy some people can be. To tear a family apart over money. I think if I had found any evidence of foul play in the book, I would throw the book in the fire and never tell anyone. I can only imagine what that family has been through.

I'm sure this book was not supposed to be left behind. I think they missed it when they were gathering up their stuff from the shed. I'm so glad to have read it, knowing the family can move on from this terrible situation they were in.

I finish eating and still have my plate on my lap from the sandwich I made. I was so into the book and couldn't put it down for a second. I just needed to finish it and see how it ended.

IT IS GETTING LATE, so I grab a cup of green tea to go look at the stars. I sit on the deck until after midnight. I am planning my next day to go to the old farmhouse I saw today. I love to explore and find different treasures. I head inside to get ready for bed. Finally, at about 1am I climb in my bed.

I fall asleep fast and wake to the bright sky and the sound of chirping birds. It is going to be a beautiful day. I get up and made coffee, then go to the deck and start my day. I am planning my little adventure to the farmhouse. *What am I going to find inside? A few bodies, skulls, old books maybe?*

I do a few things around the cabin along with my dishes. I am trying to decide what I should have for supper when I get back home. I like to plan my day before I leave the cabin. I am rushing and smash a plate on the floor as I am drying the dishes. There is glass everywhere and now I need to clean it up. I sweep twice to make sure I got all the glass picked up, then I dry the rest of the dishes and put them all away. I take out a piece of chicken for supper and make a salad to go with it. I put everything in the fridge and get ready to go.

I get dressed and make a coffee to put in my thermos cup for my adventure. Now to head out and find this farmhouse again. I lock the door and make my way to the car. I get to my car and realize I forgot my thermos, so I have to go back and grab it.

I start driving down the highway for about an hour and a half. I turn off where I think I saw the old farmhouse. The area looks familiar, so I decide to take this dirt road. As I drive a little further, I can see the old farmhouse in the distance. I am so happy to have found it on my first try and I didn't even have to drive around for hours looking. I pull over and don't see anyone around and there are no signs up. I just need to go in and check it out. I just want to look around and maybe find something interesting.

I grab my phone so I can take pictures if I need to. As I get closer, I realize it looks like it is ready to fall apart. There are 2 doors that have a latch across them. You can tell it has been vacant for years and years. I try to lift the latch. It is very heavy and rusty. I finally get the doors to open and as I enter the farmhouse, I quickly realize how creepy and dark it is in here. It doesn't have a smell, but it is so dark I can't see anything. I dig in my pocket for my cell phone and turn on the flashlight.

I start to look around to see what I can find. I see a couple of old trunks. They don't have locks on them, but they are shut. I want to open them but think I will come back to them after I look around some more. It is so creepy being in here. I can see an old wooden ladder that looks like it leads to a loft. The ladder looks homemade and is very wobbly as I touch it. I want to climb up but am scared I will fall off the old ladder. It doesn't look very safe. If I fall and get hurt, there will be nobody here to help me. I keep wandering around to see what else I can find.

I can feel webs on me as I am walking. They are everywhere. It feels like I am in a horror movie. The word creepy doesn't even begin to explain this place. The floors squeak as I walk around and I am scared I am going to fall through the floor. There are what look like horse stalls on one side of the farmhouse. I find some old shovels and pickaxes against another wall. Scanning the room, I see a couple of pitch forks there as well.

I look in every part of the farmhouse that I can until I come to an area that makes me stop in my tracks. I can see chains that are hanging from a large beam up above my head. It's obvious someone had been chained here. The chains are close together with large, old steel hand cuffs. The hand cuffs are open but still hanging off the chains. I am trying to figure out what might have happened here. It is so dark and I only have the flashlight from my cell phone.

I continue walking around to see what else I can find. I want to find my way back to the trunks I saw when I came in. I find my way back to the 2 trunks that are still sitting here. I decide to lean my flashlight against a pile of hay and position it so I can look inside. They are full of dirt and webs on the outside. I open the first one and it is very squeaky. When I look inside, I find a lot of papers. From what I can see, the papers look very old and have a rope tied around some of them. I know it will be hard to look through them in the dark. My flashlight is just a very small light so I can't see very much. I also find a few medals inside and an old army uniform. I am wondering how old this stuff must have gotten here.

I dig until I get to the bottom of the old, rusted trunk. I find a couple of coins, but they are very dirty. There isn't much more in this trunk, so I decide to go open the other one.

I open the other trunk that looks almost the same as the first one, but it is so much fuller than the other one. I start going through everything and find an old tin can. I open the tin can and find what looks like old photographs. I start to go through them and there are pictures of people hanging from chains. I think to myself, *could these be the chains I just saw on the other side of the farmhouse?* I grab my phone to shine the light on the pictures and get a closer look. I put them aside and keep on looking through the trunk. I find a few more pictures of men dressed in army uniforms, then come across an old army helmet and a pair of old boots that are tied together by the laces. There are also a couple of ripped flags and an old water canteen. The canteen has an old, shredded rope around it. I get to the bottom of the old trunk and there is just dirt and a few bullets. I put everything back inside except the tin can that is full of old pictures.

I make my way back over the other side to look at the chains that have the handcuffs attached to them. I need to see if these pictures were taken here in this farmhouse. It is hard to see with the little light I have, so I take my time. I don't want to fall through the floor. It is very creepy and the floor feels unsafe. I walk very slow until I get to the other side, where the chains and handcuffs are dangling.

I look through the tin can of pictures to see if it matches the area, I am standing next to. I need to see if anything looks familiar in the pictures that relate to the farmhouse. As I look through all the old pictures, I can see that it looks like it is indeed the right spot.

These pictures were taken here, and I feel without a doubt, that these men were hanging from handcuffs on these chains. *What did I just find and what should I do? I know I shouldn't be here, so how do I explain myself to the police?* I decide to go back to the trunks and make sure they are shut, before rushing out of the farmhouse. The trunks were close to the door, so it isn't hard to find my way out.

I get outside and have to adjust my eyes. I just came out of a dark area and now I'm in sunlight. I know I must get the doors closed and get out of here before someone comes. The barn doors are very heavy but I get them closed and use the latch to secure them. I run towards my car with the pictures I found.

I sit for a minute and have a drink of water contemplating what to do. I just want to get home and look through the pictures and see what I found. I make my way down the dirt road until I get to the highway. There is lots of cars coming, so I have to wait before I can pull out.

I put the music on and drive until I reach the cabin. I have never been so happy to be home. I park the car, grab my stuff, and go inside. I am so eager to look at these pictures I found in the old trunk. I make a coffee and sit down in my lazy boy chair. I'm not thinking of supper now. I just want to look at the pictures and find out what happened to these people and why.

I go through the pictures one by one. I can't believe my eyes. I am looking at these old photos and there are men stripped down to their underwear with handcuffs on their wrists. They are strapped to chains on both sides and their arms are spread apart. Some of the pictures have these men hanging by their hands and their feet aren't touching the ground. I think, *what was happening here? Who were these men and who did this to them?* I keep looking through these disturbing photos one by one. I get to the end of them and decide to count how many there are. I count 18 in total.

These pictures are very disturbing. The men look like they were beaten and there is blood and bruising all over them. They also show some of the men on the ground and some are in piles on top of each other. It looks like they were beaten to death, and some have what looks like bullet holes in them. These photos are very disturbing. I can't imagine what these men must have gone through. *The torture they must have encountered. They are just skin and bones.*

I get up from my lazy boy chair and now need to decide what to do about this. I know I should go to the police but I am scared to at the same time. I know I have a lot of explaining to do. I was tress passing on property even though I didn't see any signs up. I can't help but think *where are these men are now? Are they buried near that farmhouse?* I know I need to go to the police with the pictures I found.

I make another coffee and grab the salad I prepared this morning, then I go out on the deck and sit down in my chair. I listen to the birds chirping and the peacefulness that living in the country brings. I need to try and clear my mind before I head to the police station with the pictures. I sit for about an hour and decide I should make my way to town and show the police.

I go inside and put my coffee cup and bowl in the sink. I get ready, then grab my purse and the pictures before heading out the door. I leave but drove very slowly to get to town. I am trying to think of what to say and my nerves are shot. I know it is the right thing to do. I start to think, *I was just out exploring. They should understand right?*

I get gas and make my way to the police station. There is a girl at the desk. "Hi. My name is Jill, and I need to talk to someone about some disturbing photos I found" I explain to her. She tells me to take a seat and she will find someone I can talk to. I sit in a comfy chair and wait about 5 minutes. There is a tall slim officer who calls my name to come with him. I get up from my chair and walk behind him to an office. He introduces himself as, Sergeant Hill.

"What can I do for you today?" he asks.

"I was out exploring around an old farmhouse and came across something unusual" I say.

I go into details about where I was and what I came across in the old farmhouse. I tell him I didn't mean any harm; I was just there to look inside. "Here is a tin of photos I found in an old trunk" I tell him. He looks through each one of them and is studying each one slowly before going to the next one. I can see the look in his eyes as he glares at each photo. He is in shock at what he is seeing. I can see it in his eyes and body language. As he finishes looking through the photos, he looks at me and asks me if I can take him to the old farmhouse.

"I can take you there" I say.

"Wait in my office and I will go get another officer to come with us" he responds eagerly.

I sit for a few minutes, which seem like forever. I am so excited and nervous to be able to go back. I think to myself, *will I will get to look around and see if I find something I missed the first time? I really want to climb up that old ladder and look in the loft. I know it probably isn't safe, but what if the men are up there? I will take the opportunity to look, if they let me.*

I wait about 10 minutes when he comes back.

"We can leave now" he tells me.

"I forgot to mention that I have other photos on my cell phone that I took in the farmhouse." I respond.

"Can I have your cell phone to go through them?" he asks.

"Yes, of course" I say, handing it to him.

"It is very dark in the farmhouse, so you will need some bright flashlights" I tell him.

He sends the other officer to get some flashlights to take with us. The other officer comes back with 3 large flashlights. I am hoping I get one of them when we get there. They ask me to take my car and say they will follow behind me. I agree without any hesitation.

I lead the way through town and out onto the highway. I watch my speed closely. After all, I am being followed by the police. We drive not quite an hour to where I turn off. They are closely behind me as I turn onto the dirt road to where the old farmhouse is. I pull off on the side of the road as I get to the farmhouse. They pull up behind me. The officers grab the flashlights, and we make our way to the door.

The two officers lift the bar off that is across the door together with ease and we all head inside. It is still very dark, so they turn on the flashlights and hand me the other one. I take them to the area that I saw the beam and the chains hanging from it. They can also see the old handcuffs dangling from the boards. "It sure looks like something happened here" says Sergeant Hill. They are amazed at everything they are witnessing. We quickly realize this is very real. They start taking pictures of the entire area.

"Wow, this is quite the discovery" says the other officer.

"It sure is" I reply.

We head over to where the old ladder is. It is leaning up but doesn't look safe. I tell them I was wanting to go up, but was scared I might have fallen and nobody was with me at the time.

"Please head up while I hold the ladder, Kyle." Sergeant Hill says to the other officer.

"Sounds like a plan, Bill" he responds.

I ask Bill if I can go up to look around also. Bill says "if Kyle makes it up there and thinks it's safe for you, then you can go up." I agree and think this is fair.

Bill holds the old wobbly ladder as Kyle carefully makes his way to the top. He gets up there safe and sound. After about 2 minutes, Kyle yells down to Bill in a frightened voice "YOU NEED TO GET FORENSICS HERE!" I guess I'm not going up the ladder anytime soon.

Bill knows what that means and tells me it is time for me to leave the area.

"You should head back home and let us finish up here. We need to find out what is going on" says Bill.

"Would you mind if I just took another quick look around? I promise I won't touch anything," I tell him.

"it's best if you just leave, as this is now a crime scene," Bill responds politely.

I say goodbye to Kyle and Bill and make my way to the door. When I realize I have their flashlight, I go back to give it to Bill. I ask him if he would please call me tomorrow with any information on what they find. I am just curious and wish I had been able to go up the ladder. The sergeant tells me he will be in touch with me in a few days. "Thank you for all of your help. We will reach out to you soon" he says. I turn to leave when suddenly; we hear a thump and a scream. It looks like Kyle has fallen through the floor of the loft. We run over to him and he looks hurt. "My back hurts and I think I broke my leg. I need an ambulance" cries Kyle.

Sergeant Hill immediately calls for an ambulance. I stay with Kyle and talk to him, so he won't go in shock. He is hurt bad and I want to make sure he stays awake until the ambulance gets here.

"Stay with me Kyle and keep your eyes open" I say.

"I am in so much pain" he says through tears.

"I know, but the ambulance is on the way" I tell him.

It is a long drive but I need him to stay awake. Bill comes back I go to my car to grab a bottle of water and the blanket I have on my backseat. I come back and I cover Kyle up, then give him some water. Sergeant Hill heads back outside waiting for the ambulance. The ambulance driver is having a hard time finding the old farmhouse. The Sergeant decides to head down to the highway to see if he can see them. "Stay with Kyle and keep talking to him" says Bill. "I need to see where the ambulance is, so I will be back soon." He contacts them and tells them where he will be and that they can follow him here. After a few minutes, the ambulance is on scene. It seems like we have been waiting hours for them to get here.

They make their way to where we are and evaluate the situation. One of the medics goes back to the ambulance to grab the back board. They other medic does an assessment on Kyle. Kyle is in and out of consciousness. He fell from a very high spot and hit the ground hard. It doesn't take them long to load him up and get him enroute to the hospital. I can hear the sirens for a long time until they fade.

The sergeant thanks me for all my help, says he will wait for forensics to get here and will contact me with an update. I say my goodbyes and make my way to the door. I get to my car and head down the dirt road until I reach the turn to get on the highway.

I put the radio on and make my way home to the cabin. What a day this turned out to be. I just hope Kyle will be alright. He sure didn't look very good when the ambulance picked him up.

I get home to the cabin and go inside, then sit for a bit before getting up to make a coffee. I can't help but wonder if Kyle is going to be okay. I decide I will make something to eat and head to the hospital to see for myself.

I eat supper and head out to the hospital. It is still light out and there is lots of traffic. I assume people are heading home from work. I get to the hospital and ask to see Kyle. I don't have his last name, but I the nurse he is a cop and that I was there when he got hurt. I explain to her that I just want to check up on him. "Wait here and I will go get some information for you" the nice nurse tells me.

I wait about 5 minutes pacing the hospital floors until she comes back. "Follow me. He is down the hall in room 202. I will take you to him" she says. As I walk into his room, I see him laying in the hospital bed. He has a cast on his left leg below the knee. He sees me and thanks me for staying with him while waiting for the ambulance to arrive.

"Nothing is broken in my back, but I will be sore for a while. I am going to need some time to heal" Kyle tells me.

"I just wanted to make sure you were alright. You fell hard and I wasn't sure if you broke your back, and I was worried about you" I tell him.

"I should be home in a couple of days. Thanks again for staying with me" he says.

"It was my pleasure. Afterall, if it wasn't for me, you wouldn't have fallen." I reply.

After the short visit, I leave the hospital and decide to grab a coffee at Timmies before heading home. It has been a long day and I am tired.

I sit out on the deck for a few hours thinking about my day. It is all starting to make sense about the pictures I found. I have so many questions I want answers to, but have to wait for Sergeant Hill to call me.

I am thinking about what really happened in there. *Were those men tortured and then killed? Is that what Officer Kyle found up in the loft at the farmhouse? Did he find the bodies of those men?* I know it has to be bad if he called to have forensics show up. So much is going through my mind.

I know I must focus on something else for a while because my mind is racing. I just want to get to the end of this and see what really happened in the old farmhouse. I decide to give my head a rest and go inside to make a phone call.

I call my friend who lives far away, and we chat about everything and anything for a couple of hours. It's so nice to keep in touch and catch up on things. It is getting late, so we end our call around 11pm.

I run a nice hot bath to relax my body. It sure feels good. I am hoping this will help me get a good night sleep. I sit by the fire and drink a cup of hot chocolate filled with mini marshmallows, then I crawl in bed to watch a show for a bit. I shut the tv off at 1am because I need to try to get some sleep. It is so hot in the cabin, so I have to get back up and open the window.

I must have fell asleep fast because I wake up at 6am and feel like I had a good sleep. I feel rested and ready to start my day. I make coffee and go back onto the deck to enjoy the peacefulness. The birds are chirping and the sun is out.

I think today I will stay home and get some things done around the outside of my cabin. I want to pick up the old pieces of wood hanging around and burn them in the firepit. It takes all day to clean up outside, but it feels good to stay home and get some work done.

I lose track of time and when I head back inside I realize it is already 6pm and I haven't eaten yet. No wonder I am hungry. I make something to eat and finally sit down to relax. I want to go to bed early so I can go on an adventure tomorrow. I like to wake up and get out the door early enough that I can get back before dark.

I go to bed at 10pm and fall fast asleep, but wake up at 3am to open the window. It is always so hot in the cabin and I need some fresh air. I fall back asleep and wake again at 6am, Deciding to get up, I make coffee and put it in my large mug. It holds about 2 cups of coffee and lasts longer, so I'm not having to go back inside and make another one every 5 minutes.

I sit out on the deck until 9am, then go inside to get ready to go on another adventure. I'm not sure where I am headed today but know it is going to be fun. I always try to have fun on my adventures. I put a few things in my backpack and grab another coffee to go.

I don't even get all the way down my driveway when my phone rings, so I pull over to answer. It is sergeant Hill.

"We found 18 bodies up in the loft in a couple of large old trunks. We will have to have all the bodies taken out of there and try to get answers based on the pictures, along with whatever else to ID these men" he tells me.

He thanks me again, for finding the old farmhouse and taking them to it. *This may have never been found if I didn't go inside*, I think to myself.

"Thank you for calling me and giving me an update" I say.

"You are welcome, it is my pleasure." He responds before hanging up.

I make my way towards the highway for a nice, quiet drive.

I HAVE THE MUSIC on, listening to some country music. I drive for about 20 minutes and see a few vehicles on the road that pass me. It is a nice and bright sunny day for a drive. I come behind a little grey colored car. The car is going slower than the speed limit, of 100 km/hr. I stay behind the car because I'm not in a hurry to get anywhere, and I am just out to enjoy my day. I am listening to my music and just driving behind the car, when suddenly, I can see the taillight break and pieces of red glass fall on the road. *This is weird*, I think to myself. Before I have time to register what it happening, I see a foot come through the hole where the broken taillight is. I think, *what the heck is that? Is there someone in the trunk?* I keep my distance behind the car and don't get too close, but stay close enough to see that someone is obviously in the trunk.

I follow the car a little longer and now a hand comes through the broken taillight, and it is waving frantically. I now know someone is in trouble, but I don't want to alarm the driver that this is happening. I immediately pick up my cell phone and call 911. I have them on the line and tell them what is happening.

"I was following behind a car when a foot came through the taillight" I say in fear.

Someone is in trouble and I need help before I lose the car. I am no good with directions on the highway, so I need to pinpoint my location. They stay on the line with me until I can tell them the direction I am heading. I am looking for signs along the highway to give them so they know the area that I am travelling. I spot a road sign telling me the direction.

"I know what highway you are on. Are you able to give me a description of the car and the licence plate number?" the 911 operator asks.

I try to get close enough to get the plate number, but it is very dirty. I manage to give her the color of the car.

"It is a small grey Chevy Impala. It is an older type of car from what I can see" I tell her.

I give her the first 3 letters of the licence plate. That's all that I can make out because of the dirt covering it. I follow the car for another 10 minutes when it turns off to the right on a side road. I think, *this isn't good.* I tell the 911 operator the car has turned right on a dirt road. It is about 5 minutes from the last sign I saw. She says she will pass the info on to the police that are on their way.

I turn on the same road and stay way back now in case I am spotted. I can see in the distance that the car is still travelling on the dirt road. I don't think there is anything down this road, as far as houses or anything. I just keep following the car, hoping the police will arrive soon. My heart starts to race wondering what this person is doing with someone in the trunk. I know it can't be good. The time is passing and seems like an eternity. I know if the person is still in the trunk, they are a lot safer than if he stops the car. I just want the police to get here.

I ask the 911 operator if they are close. "They are about 5 minutes away" she says. I stay driving far behind and then the car comes to a stop on the side of the road. I can't stop, in case he spots me behind him. I drive slowly, passing the car as the driver is getting out. I tell the 911 operator what just happened. "The police will be there shortly, just keep driving" she assures me. I drive a little further and turn around to park for a few minutes.

I don't want anything to happen to the person in the trunk. I keep thinking I should go back and see if the car is still on the side of the road. I wait a few more minutes and the operator informs me that the police are still not there. I think, *maybe they are on the wrong road or can't find the road we turned off. This poor person won't have a chance if they don't soon get here.*

I tell the 911 operator I am heading back to see if the car is still parked on the side of the road. "Ma'am, please stay where you are" she says. Well, I know the person in the trunk is already in danger if they are in a trunk of a car. Against what I am told, I head back to where the car is parked on the side of the road.

As I get closer, I can see the car is still parked, but there is nobody here. I wasn't gone more than 5 minutes. I can't see anyone around. Suddenly, I can hear a scream coming from the woods. I park my car and tell the 911 operator the police need to get here quick. "There is screaming coming from the woods. Please tell them to hurry. This girl is in trouble and I am not about to let anything happen to her" I tell the operator.

I am thinking of a quick solution to the problem so he will come up to his car. I start blowing my horn for about 5 minutes. The screaming stops and the man appears from the woods. Just as he starts coming towards his car, I notice the police pulling up behind me. I quickly tell the police as I point to the guy, "That is the guy driving the car and he took the girl to the woods." The 2 officers get out of their car with their guns drawn.

"GET ON THE GROUND, GET ON THE GROUND!" they shout.

The man is ordered to drop to the ground. He hesitates for a minute, then realizes he has no where to go and drops to the ground as they go over and handcuff him.

As this is going on, I run through the woods making my way down the ditch. I know she isn't too far because the screams seem close. I make my way through some sharp branches and feel them cut my legs as they scratch against me. Finally, I find her with her hands tied with rope and a gag around her mouth. I take the gag off her mouth, and she is so happy to see me. I untie her hands and she gave me a hug. I tell her the police are coming and she is safe now.

One of the officers make their way down to the woods where we are and holds out a badge.

"Hi. I am Officer Wayne. We have the guy in custody and he is in the back of the police car. There is an ambulance on the way to take you to the hospital. What is your name?" he says.

"Lynne" she says.

"How did you get in the trunk of the car?" asks Officer Wayne.

"I was at the grocery store and came out to put the groceries in my car. I was grabbed from behind and thrown in the trunk of a car. I didn't see him until he stopped once and tied a rag over my mouth. I feared for my life and thought I was going to die" she says crying.

"I kicked and kicked until the taillight broke. I was just hoping someone would see my foot or hand threw the broken taillight," Lynne finishes through terrified sobs.

Lynne continues to tell the officer the guy said she is not his first abduction and wouldn't be his last. He told her he had a place to take all his girls and they never go back home. He said he has done this several times before. Officer Wayne goes on his radio to ask for back up with searching the woods. He asks the station to send a couple of officers to his location to conduct a search through the woods. Nobody knows what they are looking for, but they have to act on what Lynne told them. It's possible he has a place close by, if this is where he took her.

The officer takes Lynne up to wait for the ambulance to get here. Lynne says she is fine and just wants to go home. Her hand is bleeding from the broken glass of the taillight. The officer insists she should get checked out to make sure. She agrees to stay and wait for the ambulance, as long as I stay with her.

We talk for a few minutes, and I tell her how I saw her foot, then her hand through the taillight. I saw it on a movie once, where someone in the trunk kicked the taillight out and was saved. I tell her things might have gone differently if she didn't break that taillight. She agrees and thanks me for following the car.

After about an hour of finding Lynne, the ambulance finally shows up. The medic comes to check her over and she seems fine, other than a few marks on her wrists from the rope and a small cut from the broken taillight. She is upset and just wants to go home, not to the hospital. Lynne persists that she is fine and to please just let her go home. She asks Officer Wayne to call her husband to come get her instead of riding in the ambulance or a police car.

"Just give me your husband's name and phone number and I will call him to come meet us at the hospital," says the officer.

"I want to stay here until my husband arrives" she says, as she is trembling.

Another police car arrives, with 2 officers to search the woods in case he was taking her to a place near by. One of the first officers to arrive on scene leaves with the suspect.

Officer Wayne waits with us until Lynne's husband arrives. After about 30 minutes, Lynne's husband shows up. You can see he is in his work clothes and looks very worried about what happened to his wife. He had no trouble finding us with the directions given by the officer who called him. He wants to know how this happened and wants to make sure Lynne is alright. They hug and the officer asks Lynne to come by the station tomorrow if she is up to it to giving a statement. Her husband says he will take her there tomorrow.

Lynne and her husband leave, but I want to wait and see if the officers searching the woods find anything. Officer Wayne heads in the woods to search with the other 2 officers. I can hear them and make my way to the woods to look. I can see them down towards what looks like an old shack or shed. I hear one of the officers yell to the other officer that he found something. All 3 officers are now inside the old shack. I advance closer, hoping I can see or hear them talking. The shack looks like it is about to fall apart. It has a door, but it wasn't locked from what I can see.

I am standing outside when 2 of the officers come out.

"What are you still doing here?" asks Officer Wayne.

"I just want to see if you found anything down in the woods" I say with a slight grin.

He politely asks me to leave and thanks me for helping. One of the officers asks me to come to the station tomorrow to give a statement. I agree and leave the woods to head to my car. I take my time getting to my car to avoid scratching up my legs again. I also want to see if I can hear them talking about something they might have found.

I get in my car and think to myself, *they must have found something. Why would one yell to another officer they found something? I know there has to be something inside that shack.* I am so glad Lynne didn't get a chance to see the inside of that old run-down shack in the woods. I wait in my car for about 15 more minutes and then I leave when the officers don't come back up.

I drive with the music on low all the way home. It is still light out and the traffic is starting to get busy. I keep thinking how close Lynne came to losing her life today and I am happy I was there to help. I'm sure she was scared out of her mind, being kidnapped and put in the trunk of a car. I am just so happy she kicked out the taillight. Now I know that's what saved her life. Well, I guess I actually saved her life.

I get home after a long day and go inside to make supper, then I put on the tv to watch the news. I am wondering if there will be anything on the news about the incident today. I'm not very hungry, so I just make a chicken sandwich and a cup of tea. I sit in my lazy boy chair and put my feet up.

There is nothing on the news tonight about anything that happened today. Maybe they will have something on about it tomorrow. I make myself a coffee after supper and go out on the deck to sit and relax. It is a beautiful quiet evening. I don't want to stay up too late tonight because it was a long and stressful day. I need to remember to go to the police station sometime tomorrow and give a statement. I can't help but think, *how is Lynne doing?* She certainly had a close call today. This could have gone so differently, but I am thankful it all worked out.

I go inside after 8pm to get ready for bed. It is still early so I make a banana loaf to have with my coffee in the morning. The cabin sure smells good when banana loaf is baking. I love to bake and love the smell in the small cabin. I take it out of the oven and let it cool down before wrapping it.

The oven put some heat in the cabin, so I have to open the window for some fresh air. Now I am tired and need some sleep.

I brush my teeth and head to bed. It is time to get some sleep. I'm not sure how much sleep I am going to get, but I know I have to try and get some.

I wake at 3am, tossing and turning. I force myself to stay in bed, falling back to sleep until I wake at 7am. I feel well rested. I get up and make a cup of coffee, then head to my deck.

Quietly, I go back inside to grab my cell phone to get a few pics of the 2 deer in my yard. They look like they don't have a care in the world. They are both just standing there eating from the ground. I manage to get a few pictures until they decide they have had enough and they both wander back through the woods. I think about how it is getting late and I need to have a piece of my banana loaf with another coffee, before I get ready to go to the police station.

I finish eating, do my dishes and get dressed to go to the police station. I grab my keys, lock my door, and head to my car. I turn the radio on and head onto the highway. There seems to be a lot of traffic on the way into town today. I'm guessing people are going to work. It is a beautiful day driving with several deer sightings along the way.

I arrive at the police station at about 10am, grab my purse with my phone and head in. I stop by the desk to tell the secretary why I am here. "Take a seat and someone will be right with you," she says with a smile. After about 5 minutes, an officer from yesterday arrives. "Hi, I am Officer Moore, please follow me" he says as he shakes my hand. He is short and has a muscular build. I get up and follow Officer Moore to another room. We walk in and he shuts the door. "Take a seat and relax," he says. The room is neat and tidy with lots of pictures hanging on the walls. A bookshelf so filled you can't fit another book on it, sit on the wall facing me.

We talk for a few minutes and he thanks me for helping yesterday. We go over everything that happened, from the second I remember the car on the highway. I go into detail, step by step of everything I saw and he asks me to write it down.

"What were you thinking when you saw the taillight being kicked out?" he asks.

"Well, I knew someone had to be in the trunk" I say.

"I watched a movie and saw the same thing happen," I finish.

"You are very brave to do what you did and that's what saved Lynne's life. She may never have been found if you didn't follow them and call 911" he responds.

I tell him I did what I had to do in a bad situation.

"How Is Lynne doing?" I ask.

"I checked up on her this morning and she is still shaken up, but glad to be alive. She asked me to tell you she is grateful for everything you did yesterday," he responds.

"I am happy I was able to help" I tell him.

"Did you find anything in the old shack in the woods?" I ask.

"I can't really get into too much, but we did find evidence that people were taken there and they are still investigating the area." he answers.

I tell him I will watch the news tonight and with his eyebrows raised, he gives me a half smile. Officer Moore stands up from his desk and says "if we need anything else, we will contact you. Have a good day," then he walks me to the front door. I say "goodbye" and head out the door to my car.

I know now they found something in that old shack. I sure wish I could have gone inside to see for myself. I guess I will have to watch the news until they release something about what they found. As I am just about to get in my car, I see Lynne and her husband walking towards me. We stop and she gives me a hug, then thanks me. Her husband also thanks me and says, "she is very lucky to be alive. You are a hero."

Lynne tells me Officer Moore called her last night to inform her they had indeed found 3 other girls in that shack. They found them in a small deep freeze. They are deceased and the officers aren't sure how long they have been there. They are waiting on autopsy reports to try to get a positive ID on the 3 girls found. Officer Moore told her she is a very lucky woman and would probably have been the 4th body left in that shack had she not been located safe. I can't believe what she is telling me and how relieved I am to have followed the car that had her in the trunk. I hope this guy will be going away for life and never see the light of day again.

"You saved my life, and I will forever be grateful for that" Lynne tells me.

"I was just in the right place at the right time and I would do it all over again if I had to," I tell her as I give her a hug.

I wish her well and tell her to take care of herself, then I get in my car and leave.

I GET UP EARLY the next morning, and decide to head to town so I can treat myself to a pedicure. It sure feels good to sit and relax. I sit in a nice large, black massage chair and have a massage at the same time. I pick a beautiful bright purple color for my feet. After about an hour and a half, I am done my pedicure. I pay, then head home to the cabin to get some work done.

I drive the 20 minutes home and listen to my country music all the way. I head inside, make a coffee and grab another piece of my delicious banana loaf. I take my coffee and piece of loaf out on the deck. It is so nice outside. I want to stay on the deck all day. After my coffee and loaf, I take a walk around the yard and the trail on my property. I pick up some garbage that was laying on the ground, then head back to the cabin. I take the garbage inside, throw it in my kitchen garbage bin.

I can't believe how tired I am. I need to sit and relax in my lazy boy chair. I put the tv on and start to watch a show. It is now about 1pm in the afternoon.

I wake at 3:30pm and realize I must have fallen asleep. I can't believe how late it is. I guess if I fell asleep, I must have been tired. There is no way I am going to be able to go on an adventure today. It is getting too late, so I decide to stay home and go tomorrow. I sweep my floors and make some chocolate chip cookies. Slicing my banana loaf in half, I put the bigger piece in the freezer. It feels good to stay home and get some stuff done that I have been putting off.

I sit on the deck at about 7pm, listening to the birds. I make a cup of hot chocolate with a handful of marshmallows and sit outside until about 9pm, then I head inside to get ready for bed. I am planning to go for a hike tomorrow if I can find a place close to home. I know there are a few places I want to check out.

I have a good night sleep and wake at 7am. It is so peaceful and a beautiful day for an adventure. I get ready to venture out for a drive. I get dressed, make a peanut butter sandwich and wrap a piece of banana loaf to take. My backpack is heavy with lots of cold water and it is now time to leave, so I can find a trail or dirt road to take. I always hope to find one that I haven't been on before.

I get in my car and head down the highway. I drive for about a half hour, before coming to a road that looks interesting. It has 2 large painted rocks on one side and a large old barrel on the other. *Well, this is definitely the road I am taking today*, I think to myself. I turn off the highway and make my way down. I drive for about 10 minutes when I see another dirt road to take. I turn onto the other dirt road and keep driving for about 10 more minutes. I can see a huge pile of rocks that are stacked up very high. I want to go try to climb them and get some pictures. I just hope I can find my way back to the highway after all this.

I pull up as close to the rocks as I can. I can't believe how high they are piled. I get out of my car and holding my cell phone I contemplate climbing the rock pile. I just don't want to fall, because there is nobody around to help me if I fall off the rocks and get hurt.

I switch from my sandals, to socks and sneakers so I can climb up easier. After a few minutes I start to climb. It is high and I am having a blast. I get so far up the rocks and decide to stop and take a few pictures. I need to be so careful not to fall, so I sit on a rock. The rocks start to move as I get up to climb higher. Now I am thinking, I shouldn't climb up but instead, should start heading back down.

As I start to make my way back down, the rocks start to fall. I get scared because I don't want to get crushed or hurt. The more I climb down, the more the rocks keep falling. They are going in every direction and falling fast. I jump from rock to rock as careful as I can without falling to the ground.

I finally make it safe on the ground but there are rocks everywhere. I am so glad I didn't fall and that I got some awesome pictures while up on the rocks. I go over to my car to grab a bottle of water, then I sit on the rocks that fell. I stay there a few minutes and drink my water. I turn my head and notice what looks like a hollow hole through the rocks. As I get a closer look, I can see light in behind the pile of rocks. I put my water bottle down and start taking the rocks off the pile one by one. There are still so many rocks to move and they are too heavy for me to lift. I try and try but they won't budge. I know I can crawl through the little opening, but at the same time don't want to get trapped in there.

I make sure I have my cell phone and my bottle of water, as I head through the tiny opening. I am wondering what could be on the other side of these rocks. I manage to climb through and land on the other side. It is dark but I am able to move some more rocks from the inside. They are so heavy, but some just start to fall. The opening gets bigger and bigger as the rocks continue to fall. I can't help but think, *what is in here? Where am I and what am I going to find? I hope it is something interesting. Like bodies, or skeletons.* It is so dark, but I keep walking and walking. I hope nothing jumps out at me. I have found a cave from what I can tell. The walls are all rock and some have paintings on them. It looks like they have been spray painted over the years. I don't see any dates, just some names and pictures. I keep walking and looking around to see what else I can find. I come across a big pile of blankets and pillows that look very old and smell stinky. I think they must have been here for years. *What is this place and who did these belong to?* I take a few pictures but I'm not sure if they will turn out very good, because it is so dark in here.

I continue to look around and it seems like I am walking for miles when I come across a few old tires and some steel rails. I'm not sure why these things are here and still don't know what this place is, other than a cave of some sort. There is so many paths to take, so I think I will just take one way at a time and see what I can find. I am hoping I don't get lost. I don't think there would be any cell service in here.

I keep wandering around and find some different things to indicate someone was obviously here before. I am trying to figure out why the rocks were piled to cover the cave up. I would never have found this place if the rocks hadn't fallen. I keep looking around until I find what looks like a skeleton. I look closer to make sure, and it is in fact a skeleton. It is in the corner and half covered with a dirty old blanket. I can see the upper half but know instantly, that it is human remains. I want to keep looking inside the cave in case there are more remains here. I go a little further and find a couple more bodies that are leaning against a wall. They have what looks like rope around their ankles and are also wearing clothes that look like rags. They must have been here for many years.

I continue looking around the cave and find some old chains and a few rusty old water cans. I also find shoes and pieces of clothing that were thrown to one side of the cave. I find what looks like dog leashes and collars. *Could these people have been caged up like animals? What the hell* I thought. *Who would do this and what happened here?* I know I need to get some help and tell the police about the cave. I need to leave and go to the police. I want to keep looking but it is creepy. I don't think anyone will find me here because the cave is covered up so well.

I make my way, hoping to find the entrance of the cave, so I can go get help. After about 20 minutes, I find the opening again. I don't want to leave so I decide to just call the police while sitting on the rocks and tell them about the cave. I get put through to an Officer Smith. I introduce myself and tell the officer what I have found. I don't think he really believes me at first and must think he has a crazy person on the phone. As I continue to tell him about what I have discovered, he asks me where I am and I to try my best to give him directions to the cave. As I tell him my whereabouts, he stops me.

"I am familiar with the area and can find the place. I want you to wait there for me and I will get another officer to come with me," he announces.

"I am not going anywhere" I say.

We both hang up and I wait for the officers to arrive. I wait about 45 minutes, when my phone rings.

"This is Officer Smith. Can you tell me which dirt road you took when you got off the highway?" he says in a deep voice.

I try to explain to him which one I took but he sounds confused.

"I am at the turn off on the highway" he tells me.

"Stay there and I will come find you" I respond.

"Okay great! I will wait for you," he answers, relieved.

I get in my car and drive about 20 minutes before I can spot the police car. I pull up and wave to the officers to follow me. When we arrive, I pull over and stop the car, then get out. The officers also get out of their car and introduce themselves as Officer Smith and Officer Hines. Officer Smith is over 6 feet tall with a slim build and Officer Hines is not quite 6 feet with a heavier build.

"What are you doing here and how did you find the cave?" asks Officer Smith.

"I was out exploring, as I do quite often, and started to climb up the rocks to take some pictures. Suddenly, some rocks fell and that's when I saw the opening. I decided to go see what was behind the rocks. I went inside and that's when I found skeletons and other stuff, so I knew I had to call you guys," I answer.

The 2 officers make their way through the opening and I follow behind them so I can show them the skeletal remains I have found. It is dark as we enter and we can't see much. I just want to get back inside to see what else I can find. They ask me which way, so I say "go left". After a few minutes of walking around we come across the first skeleton. I tell them to keep going as there is more up further. They can't believe their eyes at what's in front of them. They didn't even know this cave existed. It is dark and we only have flashlights to be able to look around. There is no way of telling how many human remains are in this cave.

We keep looking and find a few old lanterns and some buckets that are all rusty. We find ropes and chains.

"These bodies must have been here for decades" says Officer Hines.

"Agreed. We will need to leave the cave and call-in forensics to come investigate. These remains need to be taken for an autopsy to get more information" says Officer Smith.

They will have to through the cave step by step and make sure there aren't anymore skeletal remains in here.

All 3 of us make our way back to the entrance of the cave. We climb through the opening to where it is daylight. Officer Smith goes to his police car and calls this in. I wait by the rocks with Officer Hines. Officer Smith comes back to tell us there is a group of 6 coming in to explore the cave and get the human remains out to be examined. We talk for a few minutes about how coming across this cave was nothing but pure luck. If I hadn't been out on an adventure today, this cave might never have been found.

Officer Smith takes all my information and tells me I can leave but they will be in touch with me. I ask him if I can stay but he insists I leave and head home. I want to stay and go back inside the cave. I want to see what else they find when the rest of them get here. The officer is persistent that I must leave the area, so I say my goodbyes and get in my car to leave.

I turn my radio on and head towards the highway. The road is long and dirty with lots of trees on both sides. As I am getting to the end of the dirt road to turn onto the highway, I can see 2 more police cars heading in the direction of the cave. I wish I could have stayed to see what else they find. This is so exciting and I just want to be a part of it. I have so many questions. *How long have the remains been there and who did this?*

It takes me about an hour on the highway before I get home. There is so much traffic going in the same direction as me. I keep thinking about the rock pile and how I found the cave. I am glad I went inside it to explore and found the remains. I hope they can identify them. It might be impossible if they have been there for decades. I think of how creepy it was standing next to a skeleton. Ewe, Ewe, Ewe!

I go inside the cabin to make a coffee, before sitting out on the deck. It is a beautiful evening, and I had a very long day. My legs are sore from climbing up the rocks. I am just glad I didn't fall when the rocks started tumbling down. I am going to call Officer Smith in the morning to find out if anymore evidence was found. I can hardly contain my excitement.

I go inside the house and make some supper. I am craving fish and chips, so that's what I decide to make. I put it in the oven and turn the tv on. It takes about 40 minutes before my supper is done. It smells so good. I sit down to eat and relax, while watching tv. The news is on but there is nothing about the cave. I really don't think there will be anything on the news tonight. It is too early and they are probably not finished their investigation.

I finish supper and do my dishes before I make a hot chocolate and go out on the deck. It is about 7pm and the stars are out. The sky is lit up and I can see the big dipper. It's so peaceful looking at the stars in the sky. I sit out on the deck just about every night before I go to bed. I think the fresh air helps me sleep. When I decide to go to bed, it takes me a long time to fall asleep, but I have always been a problem sleeper.

I go inside and get ready for bed, then I watch a few shows and finally decide to shut the tv off at 10pm. I want to try to get some sleep and rest my sore tired legs. It doesn't take me too long to fall asleep, but I wake up to open the window. It's 1am and the cabin is so hot. I need some fresh air. I fall back to sleep and wake at 6am. I feel well rested, but my legs are still sore from climbing the rocks.

I need to quickly make a coffee and get ready to head to the police station to talk with Officer Smith. I'm not about to wait for him to call me about the findings in the cave. I drink my coffee and make a piece of toast, along with a banana. I get dressed and head on my way for the 20-minute drive to town. I stop to get gas, before arriving at the station. I go inside and ask at the front desk if I can speak to Officer Smith.

"Officer Smith is not in the office right now. Is there someone else I can get to help you?" She asks.

"Can I see Officer Hines?" I ask.

"Sorry, he is not in the office either" she responds.

"Thank you. I will just come back later," I say and proceed to my car.

I am pretty sure I know where both officers are. I am going to the cave to see for myself if they are there. I head back towards the highway that leads to the cave. I know it will take me over an hour to get there. I turn the radio on and hit the highway. The traffic is slow and the weather is sunny. I get to the turn off, with the dirt road and continue on to where the cave is.

As I turn onto the dirt road, I can see several police cars and a white van heading towards me. I figure they must have come from the cave and have taken out some remains. I keep driving until I reach the area. I park and wait in my car to see what they are doing. I can see so many people and police cars. I am trying to see if I can find Officer Smith, so I can get out and talk to him. After a few minutes, I finally see Officer Smith come out of the cave. I wait to see where he is going. He heads towards a police car not too far from my car, so I decide to get out and talk to him. He is not shocked to see me and just grins.

"Did you find any more remains?" I ask him.

"So far, we have found 18 bodies but we are still not done looking through the cave. We are looking for any evidence of who might have done this and why these people are here. The bodies will have to be removed and sent to the lab for analyses" says a very tired looking Officer Smith.

"We won't have anymore news until the remains are examined to determine the cause of death and the estimated year of death. What we do know, is the bodies have been here for many years. We will be here for the next couple of days to make sure we don't miss anything and every bit of evidence is taken out of the cave. I am leaving now for a few hours but will be back later today. I will keep in touch with updates; however, you need to let us do our jobs and this information needs to remain confidential until the investigation is closed." Office Smith tells me.

I agree and get back in my car to head towards the highway. I am glad I went back to the cave to see what progress they are making. I get to the turn for the highway and head back home. Well, at least that's where I think I am headed. I take a few turns off the highway leading down some more dirt roads. I manage to get some pictures before I make my way to the cabin. It is still early so I think I will go home and go for a nice long walk.

I get home and make a grill cheese sandwich and sit on the deck to eat it with a bottle of water. It is a beautiful day and I didn't want to waste it by sitting at home. I quickly eat my sandwich, then go inside to get ready. I put my runners on and grab my cell phone. I forgot to charge my phone so it won't be long before it goes dead.

I go for a 2km walk. There is lots of traffic on the road. It's a dirt road and pretty dusty, so I decide to turn around and head back. I don't want to play any music because my phone is almost dead. I get home and feel so dirty from the dust that I have to run the water for a bath. I plug my phone in to charge it up. My legs are still sore and the hot steaming bath feels so soothing. My mind is still thinking about the cave and skeletons I found. *Imagine, what they must have gone through to die that way.*

After my bath, I make a hot chocolate and put the tv on to watch the news but it is over after 15 minutes, so I watch a few shows instead. It is getting late and I decide to go out on the deck for about an hour before I head to bed. I need to try to get some sleep but my thoughts keep me awake. I don't know when I finally doze off. The next morning at about 10am my phone rings.

"This is Officer Smith" says the voice on the other end.

"I am letting you know that we are done at the cave. We found 22 bodies in total and they are being sent out to find out how they died" he says.

"Wow, that's a lot of bodies" I tell him.

"It sure is. I will be in touch once I have more information" he tells me.

"Thank you and I look forward to talking with you again" I respond before hanging up.

Several weeks later...

I decide to give Officer Smith a call to see if there is any new information.

"Hello Jill, what can I do for you today?" he says when he answers.

"Hi Officer Smith, I am calling to see if there are anymore updates?" I ask him.

"Well, we have decided to block the cave off to ensure no one tries exploring it. We don't know how stable it is and can't risk someone finding it and getting hurt. As for the skeletal remains, it may take months or years before we have any new information. This is going to be a difficult case to solve and we may never get the answers we hope for," he replies.

"Understandable. I was wondering why the news didn't mention the cave. Thank you for keeping me updated. I am still struggling with what I found and was hoping for more answers." I tell him.

"We are all hoping for the same Jill. In the meantime, if you are ever in need of help, please ensure you speak with your doctor or other health care professional," he says.

"I will. Thank you." I answer.

"Take care, Jill." He says before hanging up.

I MAKE A COFFEE and decide to go out on the deck. I feel relieved that they are done at the cave and can hopefully find out what happened in there. This has really affected me, more than I thought. I keep picturing the human remains I saw in the cave and I'm now having nightmares. I am not going on an adventure today. I need to stay home and try to take my mind off everything I have been through the last little while. I just want to keep busy and try to forget the images in my head.

One month later...

My nightmares seem be getting better, but they are keeping me up at night. I make an appointment with my doctor to see if maybe she can give me something to help me sleep. It takes a week to get in to see her. We talk about everything that is bothering me. "I am going to try you on a pill for depression instead of a sleeping pill" she says. I try to explain to her I am not depressed, but she insisted that's what I need and that it will also help me sleep.

I go to the pharmacy to get the prescription filled and start taking them right away, but I toss and turn and still can't get to sleep. Now, I'm beginning to feel shaky all day long. These pills are not helping.

I call the doctor to let her know how the pills make me feel. "I need you to stay on the pills and give them time to work" she says. I agree to keep taking them a little longer to see if they will make me feel better in time.

I stay on the pills for about another week and I am still having nightmares and waking up with the shakes. It is getting so bad I don't feel safe. I don't even want to drive anywhere anymore. Daily, my head feels like it is going to explode and the nightmares are getting worse. Night after night, I suffer until I have to do something about it. I need to commit myself to the psych ward at the hospital. I don't want to call the doctor again, so I make my own decision. This is the right thing to do.

I pack a bag and take my pills with me, then drive myself to the hospital. I know I need help and maybe this is the way to get the help I need. On my way to the hospital, which is about 20 minutes, I keep seeing things jump in front of me and slow down, because I worry that I hit something. My mind is giving me such mixed feelings. It takes me over an hour to get to the hospital and by the time I get there I am shaking and wiping my tears away. *What is happening to me?* I think to myself. I park my car, grab my bag and go inside to check in.

I make my way through the doors and down the hall following the psych ward signs. I walk slow and feel like I am moving from side to side, all the way to the desk to check myself in. The lady asks if she can help me. I tell her "I don't feel good, and I am checking myself in." She comes around the side I am on and gets me a chair to sit in. We go over the reason I think I need to be here and she asks a ton of questions. "Are you taking any medication, street drugs or alcohol?" she asks me. I give her the bottle of pills I am taking and tell her I have the occasional drink.

After doing some paperwork and having me sign it, she escorts me down the hall in a wheelchair and places me in a room. The room has a twin sized bed, a nightstand, dresser and a tv hung on the wall. The bright mauve curtains hang on the windowsill. The bedspread is a bright yellow. I notice these colors because they make the room look so bright and safe. I start to feel calm and under the impression that she cares. "Make yourself comfortable and a doctor will be in to see you in a few minutes to go over some more stuff" she tells me with a smile. She shows me where I can put my clothing in the dresser or closet if I want.

I get settled in as much as I can and sit on the bed waiting for the doctor to get to my room. The doctor comes in and introduces himself as Dr. Tom. He calls me by my name, as he is looking at the paperwork I filled out when I arrived. He pulls up a chair and we talk for about a half hour.

"Do you feel suicidal or have any other thoughts of hurting yourself?' he asks.

"No" I say.

"I just feel weird ever since I have started taking these pills." Then I show him the bottle.

"What is the reason you were put on these pills?" he asks, taking the bottle from me and looking it over.

I tell him about the cave and finding the skeletal remains, along with how much effect this has had on me.

"I have been having nightmares and shaky feelings ever since," I inform him.

"Well, you will be safe here. We will make sure you are comfortable" he assures me.

He tells me over and over this is a safe place to be. We end the conversation and he leaves me with a schedule of meetings that will be helpful, along with a meal plan. He says the meetings are for me to see what everyone in here is going through and to try to help each other in difficult times. He also states I can attend the meetings and just sit and listen if I want. There is no pressure to talk but just to listen to others. "Again, I am Dr. Tom and if there is anything you need, please feel free to ask," he says, as he walks out of the room. He leaves my room and I stay seated on the bed.

I sit thinking for over an hour, wondering if I made the right decision coming here. I feel like I did because it has made me feel safer. I watch as people are going up and down the hall. A few people pass my room and look in. Some people wave and some of them smile. Others just keep walking past.

I slowly get up from the bed and close my door. I just want to lay down and rest. It is too quiet so I turn the tv on low and find the country music channel. I love my country music because it helps me relax. I look at the time on my cell phone and it is 2pm. I lye down on the bed and try to rest. I toss and turn before eventually falling asleep. I wake up to the sound of people in the hallway and the clock tells me it's 4:30. I can hear noises outside my door and think it must be suppertime. I am not hungry and don't feel like being around anyone, so I stay in my room with the door shut.

At about 6pm there is a knock on my door. I ask who it is.

"My name is Anne, and I am a worker here," she answers.

"Come in," I tell her.

"Hello" she says, bringing me a tray of food.

I tell her I am not hungry; I am just tired. "Please, just try to eat something on the tray. The food here is good and the dessert is even better," she says. *It might make me feel better to eat some food*, I think. She stays in my room and says "if there is anything you need, you can just come out to the desk. There is a large game room all set up with a large tv and some puzzles if you want to go look." I tell her I might try a little later but don't want to leave my room right now. I ask her to just please leave me alone and thank her for the tray of food. She leaves my room and leaves the door wide open. I quickly get up and close the door. I just want to be alone.

It is now about 9pm and the halls are quiet. I leave the tv on the music channel and get dressed into a pair of sweatpants and a tank top. I eat some jello that is on my tray, drink some juice and lay back on the bed. At about 10pm someone knocks on my door.

"It's Anne, are you awake?" she says in a quiet voice.

"Yes, come in." I answer.

She is checking on me to see if I ate anything and brought me my pill to take.

"Is there anything you need before bed because it is lights out at 11pm?" She tells me.

"No, but thank you. I just want to get some sleep," I tell her.

She gives me my pill and watches me take it. Then, she takes the tray and leaves the room, leaving the door open. After she leaves, I get up, close the door and take the pill out of my mouth to flush it down the toilet. There is no way I am taking these pills anymore. I don't think they are working, but instead think they are making me crazy! I crawl in bed and fall asleep after midnight.

I wake up at 6am after having a restless sleep. I get up and brush my teeth, then get changed. I can hear people outside in the hall. It's 8am and I'm hungry. I open my door and peak out. There is a young lady walking in the hall.

"Hello" she says, as she walks by.

"Hello" I respond, as I walk to the kitchen.

The kitchen has about 15 people sitting down eating and drinking coffee. I go get a coffee and take a seat. After a few minutes, the lady I saw in the hall asks if she can sit with me. I say yes and tell her my name. "My name is Gail" she says. We talk for a few minutes, before I decide I want to go back to my room.

At 10am, the nurse comes to my room with my pill. She watches me take it, then leaves. Only this time, she closes the door. I go to the bathroom and flush it down the toilet again.

One week later...

The nightmares are starting to go away and I am feeling like my old self again, but I want to stay in the ward until I feel good enough to leave. I head to the games room to see if there is a puzzle I can do. I always find one and will sit for hours doing it. The games room always has so many people in there doing something.

As I am working on my puzzle, I overhear 2 people talking about how people are dying in the facility. They say this place has had 5 deaths in the last 2 months. I think maybe there were all suicides and think nothing of it, until they say the deaths were all drug overdoses. *Well, how can it be drug overdoses when there are not allowed any drugs in here?* I think to myself. I continue to listen in, while pretending to do the puzzle and the 2 of them are just rambling on. They say the police are suspecting a staff member is doing the killings, but they have no proof.

The 2 guys leave the room and I decide to go see Gail to ask her if she knows anything about this. She tells me she heard about this shortly after she arrived here 3 weeks ago. There have been unexplained deaths, that are confirmed to be drug overdoses. We talk for a few minutes before I go back to my room. I want to try to find out more on my own.

I start asking the staff questions and the doctor that I am seeing. They all say they have no idea, but it is confirmed to have been drugs that killed all 5 people at this facility. The staff at the facility don't want to continue talking about this, so they change the subject every time it is brought up.

It is late afternoon and I am in the game room doing a puzzle. There are just a few people in there, so I discreetly make my way over to the 2 people I overheard talking about the 5 deaths. I introduce myself and so do they. We talk for a few minutes and I ask them what they heard about the deaths in here. They both say they were told it was drug overdoses for all 5 victims. They both continue playing their board game, so I wander off down the hall. I am trying to see who works here, get some names and info on each one. I am just asking general questions when I talk to them, to find out as much personal information as I can. I start thinking, *what if it is a staff member killing people off? How else could this be happening?* I try a new strategy when talking to the staff and doctors, to see if I can catch them in a lie or if they are hiding something.

I take notes about all my conversations with them and keep them under my mattress, continuing to flush my pills down the toilet. I have been here for 3 weeks now and I feel back to normal. I am not having any more nightmares and feel so much stronger, but I don't want to tell them how I feel because now I have work to do. I need to try to find out why these people are dying.

I spend so much time around the staff and trying to fit in, but also letting them think I am still having problems and need to be here longer. It is getting late and I head to my room at 8pm. The nurse comes in at 10pm with my pill. She watches me take it and after she leaves, I take it out of my mouth. I realize just as it falls into the toilet that it is a different pill than the original one, I was taking. I can't figure out why I am on a different pill and nobody told me. *How long have they been giving me this pill and who switched me without telling me?* This is my right to know. This is my body and my health. Now I start to wonder if this is what's going on around here. Maybe we are getting the wrong drugs and people are dying from it. From here on out, I am saving all the pills I am given and putting them in a bag.

There is no name on the pill but there is a letter T. I try to google it but don't have any luck. After about a week of seeing what staff come in and out, I realize there is a male staff that only works 3 times a week. I start to focus on him because he is very quiet and doesn't interact with any one of us. He stays to himself and keeps his distance. This makes me suspicious and I want to get closer to him, so I decide to find him and ask some personal questions about where he's worked before this place and if he has family. He doesn't tell me much but does tell me where he used to live. I don't get his last name, but I know I can find out what it is.

His shift is from 4 to 12 in the evening, 3 times a week. Although, if someone calls in sick, he will fill in for them. With an uninterested expression, he asks me if I have any family. We only have a brief conversation before he walks away. I find that very strange for someone who is supposed to be here to support all of us. It seems like he has no interest at all in working here.

I continue following him around, trying not to be noticed. Every time he works, he comes into our rooms with meds, which I continue to save. He is paying more attention to people who seem like they need help and are isolating themselves from the world. I start to notice he is spending more time in some rooms than others.

I get up one morning and ask Dr. Tom if I can get a day pass to go home and get some items. It seems like he cares about all of us. He gives me permission to go for 3 hours and has me sign a release form stating that I can go from 12 to 3pm. I can sign myself out and leave anytime, but feel like I still need to be here. At least, that's what I'm making them think.

I get ready and head home to the cabin for a few hours. I want to look up the pill I am suppose to be taking, to see if I can get any info on it. I also try to find out any information on the male worker that works 3 days a week. I don't have much luck on getting information on either. I get some stuff I need and grab my laptop to take, then I head back to the hospital. I arrive back at 2:50pm, go to my room to put all my stuff away and plug in my laptop. I set it up on a small table by my bed.

At about 4pm, I enter the game room and overhear someone talking about another death here. They found a male dead in his room at ten this morning. I can't believe what I am hearing. *Why are so many people dying here?* I start to worry and think *maybe I should leave*. I just really want to see if I can find out how they are dying. I start to panic and think *maybe I can get the pill to the police and see if they can get it analyzed. What if they think I am crazy?*

I get the names of everyone working here, including all the doctors and even the staff working the desk. I need to get to the bottom of this. I have my laptop now, so I can try to google everything I can about the staff. I spend a lot of time over the next few days in my room trying to see if I can find anything on the staff. It is hard to look up people if you don't know where they are from or where they worked before this place. *Is this the reason these people are not getting any better? If I can't find any information on anyone, then I don't think the people hiring can either,* I think to myself.

I am still not having any luck, so I look up different psych wards to see if they have any familiar cases of unexplained deaths. Now I know I am getting somewhere. After hours of searching the internet, a psych ward pops up with seven unexplained deaths that are coming back as drug overdoses. This is the same type of thing that seems to be happening here. This isn't coincidental. *Or is it?* This facility is in Canada. I continue looking at picture after picture of this facility. They have pictures of the outside, around the grounds. They have a beautiful garden and lots of places to sit. There is a huge water fountain to sit by. It continues to show pictures of the inside which includes the kitchen and a couple of game rooms. It also shows the inside of the bedrooms. The place looks beautiful. At the end of the all the pictures it shows the staff and doctors that work, or have worked there over the years. I just briefly scroll though them until I see someone that catches my eye.

I had to take another look at the picture, because I can't believe what I am starring at. It is a picture of Dr. Tom. He is a doctor that worked at this faculty. I think, *Am I seeing things or is this for real?* The only thing is, in this picture the Dr. Tom that I know, is called Dr. Ryan. *Is it a twin brother or is it a doctor in disguise?* I now have somewhere to go with this. I need to continue watching Dr Tom, or whatever his real name is. I can't go to the police without any hard evidence. This is just not enough to go by and could be nothing to worry about. Although, my gut tells me otherwise. A real doctor wouldn't have different names. There is something fishy going on here and I will figure it out.

I take pictures of everything I find and save it all in a file on my laptop. I need proof that this doctor is killing people off, or slowly drugging them to make it look like they overdosed. This makes me think about why they are giving me a different pill when I arrived at the facility. I am so glad I decided to stop taking the pills and saved some of them.

I need to think about what I should do next. I am afraid this Dr. Tom is an imposter and is hurting people, leading to their deaths. The big question is, how to prove it. I need proof and don't want to make accusations without any type of proof to back me. I need to sit and think hard about what my next step should be. I stay in my room and continue looking at the pictures from the other facility Dr. Tom worked at. I decide to make a phone call to the facility he worked at and ask to speak to him. I want to know what they will say or the reason he no longer works at that facility. It is getting late and I want to wait and call in the morning. At this time, it is 7pm and I have missed supper.

I need to have a coffee and a piece of toast from the kitchen. We are allowed to go have a light lunch or snack if we get hungry. I shut my door and head down the hallway to the kitchen. I pass a few people in the hall and there are others in the game room. I get to the kitchen and pour a coffee and put a couple slices of rye bread in the toaster. Anne enters the kitchen to see who is in there. She says she heard someone and wanted to make sure they were ok. I tell her I slept through supper and I am hungry, so I came for toast and a cup of coffee. She says it's fine and asks me how I am feeling since being in the facility. I tell her "I am doing great and this place is really helping me, but I am still not ready to leave yet."

She leaves to answer the phone that we can hear ringing at her desk and says she will be right back. She is working the desk and doesn't want to miss any calls in case it is an emergency. My toast is ready, so I smear it with peanut butter and sit down to enjoy my toast and coffee. After about 5 minutes, Anne comes back and asks if she can sit with me. I say "absolutely!" We make small talk and I decide to mention Dr. Tom and how I feel about his great personality. I want to get her reaction, or thoughts on him. I need to see if she has anything good, or bad to say about him but don't think she will say anything. She does tell me he has been only working here at this facility for about 8 months. I ask her if he has any family. "He is very private and keeps to himself. I don't think he has a drivers license, but he must live close because he walks everywhere and he is never late" she says. She hears her phone ringing at the desk again and says she needs to go and will talk to me later. I finish my toast and grab an orange as I leave the kitchen with my coffee in hand.

I go to my room, sit on my bed with my laptop and continue trying to find information about Dr. Tom, or Dr. Ryan. I'm not sure at this point who he really is. At 10pm I hear a knock on my door.

"Who is it?" I ask.

"It's Anne, may I come in?" She asks me.

I turn my laptop the other way and tell her to come in. She says it is time to take my pill but she can't stay to chat because she has others to tend to. She leaves after she watching me take my pill and I immediately take the pill out of my mouth and put it in the bag with the rest of them. Turning my laptop back around, I continue looking for more information on the 7 deaths at the other facility where Dr. Tom worked. I want to see if there if there is a connection. The only thing I know for sure is that it is the same cause of deaths there, as it is at this facility. I stay on my laptop for hours until I can't keep my eyes open anymore. It is getting late and I need sleep. At 1am I close the laptop and try to get some sleep.

I wake up at 7am to noise in the hallway. I quickly get up, get dressed and head to the kitchen for coffee. There are about 10 people in the kitchen having breakfast. I just get a coffee and take it back to my room. I want to get back on my laptop and continue finding out what I can on Dr. Tom. I need to have a lot more evidence if I am going to go to the police.

I drink my coffee and scroll through the internet looking for whatever I can find. At 10am, I hear a knock on my door. "It's Dr. Tom, can I come in?" My heart starts to race but I know I need to be calm when he enters my room. I turn the laptop around and close it. I tell Dr. Tom to come in. He hands me my pill that is in a little clear small cup. He gives me a drink of water and watches me swallow it.

"How are you doing and is there anything you need?" he asks politely.

"I am fine, but just a little tired," I say.

I don't want him to stay too long and I need to spit the pill out before it melts in my mouth. He says goodbye and leaves my room. I spit the pill out and add it to my collection, that I am saving in a bag.

I don't want anyone else to die and what I really need to do is go to the police and tell them everything. The first thing I need to do before I go to the police is to call the other facility Dr. Tom worked at. I make sure my door is shut tight and put the tv on low, so nobody can hear me talk on the phone. I take a deep breath and decide to call and get whatever information I can about this so-called Dr. Ryan.

It is 10:30 and probably a good time to call the other facility. I get out my paper and a pen so I can write everything down, if I get information at all about this Dr. Ryan. I take a deep breath. I am trying to figure out what to say and how to start the conversation. I need to say I am a concerned worker from another facility and having issues with Dr. Tom. I just need to make sure I say Dr. Ryan when I call, so it doesn't look suspicious.

I sit back in my chair and dial the phone number. After about 3 rings a lady answers. "Hello, my name is Lillian, how may I help you?" she asks in a soft voice. I tell her my name and that I am looking to talk to someone in charge. She connects me to the supervisor. The supervisor introduces herself as Helen. I tell her my name and say that I am calling from another facility to talk about Dr. Ryan. The phone goes silent and then she asks "what do you need to know?" I talk about Dr. Ryan and how he is working at the facility I work at now. She asks what my concerns are and how she can help me.

We talk and I tell her we have had 5 deaths at this facility and another one the other day. They were all drug related. I ask her how long he worked there for and if they had any issues with him. She tells me that Dr. Ryan worked at their facility for 3 years before he quit. The reason he quit was because he was a suspect in an ongoing investigation regarding the deaths at the facility.

"We had no proof he did anything, other than he was caught giving a patient a pill that the patient wasn't on. He covered himself by saying he didn't have his glasses on and read the name on bottle wrong. The case was thrown out of court and the deaths were considered drug overdoses. They could never prove he had anything to do with the deaths. The court couldn't hold him accountable for any involvement with the deaths and there was no proof he contributed to them, so he was never charged" she responds.

"Oh wow! Does he have any family around here? Maybe married or kids?" I ask her.

"He is a very private person. Never talked about family. He never went to any staff outings or parties we invited him to. He kept to himself with no involvement with anyone outside the office. We respected that and left him alone," she says.

I thank her for the information and ask her if I can call back if I need more information on him later. She tells me I can call at anytime. We hang up and now I know this guy is involved with these deaths, but I need to figure out how.

I know I need to go to the police and hope they believe me. I have so much information written down and now he works at another facility using a different name. Just that alone is considered to be using an alias and he can and should be charged. At least I would think he should be charged. I want to have everything I need before I go to the police so they will take me seriously.

I have all this new information and now I know its time to go to the police with everything I have. I make sure to write everything down, including the name of the other facility this Doctor worked at before. I need to try to get another day pass and I need it now! I quickly get dressed and go see Dr. Tom about getting a day pass for a few hours. I am trying to figure out an excuse as to why I need another day pass, after just having one.

I go down the hall to see if Dr. Tom is in and I am told by the kitchen staff that he is in his office. I make my way down the long narrow hall to see him. His door is open, so I knock lightly and see him sitting at his desk on his computer. He says "come in," without looking up. I enter and say my name then ask Dr. Tom if I can get a day pass to go get a few personal items I forgot to get when I was out a few days ago. He says he has no problem giving me another day pass if that's what makes me happy. I kind of think that is a little weird but don't say anything. I just want the pass so I can go to town and head to the police station with all my information on this doctor.

I leave his office after signing the day pass which is for 3 hours. It is from 1 to 4. I have a few hours to waste before I can leave, so I decide I am going to put these hours to good use. I go to the kitchen to make a coffee and head back to my room.

I sit on my bed with the laptop and start searching for anything else I can find on this doctor. I want to know where he lives and where he worked before these 2 facilities. I'm not having any luck finding out anything else on this doctor. I need to expand my search and think, *is there something about the court case from the other facility?* Dr. Ryan did go to court and was never charged, so maybe the case was in the newspaper.

I search and search until I find an article about a doctor acquitted on all charges in deaths at a local facility. I continue reading this and realize it is all about Dr. Ryan working at the other facility. I have another piece of the puzzle to take and show the police. I don't have access to a printer at the facility I am at, but write the name of the article down so I can find it again. I also take a few pictures of the screen on my laptop from my cell phone. I put everything together and pace the floor until it is time to go to the police station. The time seems to drag on, so I go to the kitchen to get something to eat. My stomach is growling and I need food.

I make my way down the hall and into the kitchen. The kitchen is empty, so I just make a piece of toast and put peanut butter on it. I pour a glass of juice from the fridge and sit down to eat. I don't realize how hungry I am until I start eating my toast. It is almost noon and other people are coming in to wait for lunch to be ready. I clean off the table I am sitting at and head back to my room.

I sit on the bed and think about what I am going to tell the police. I just hope they will believe me and investigate this doctor. I put some papers in a bag and close my laptop. I want to take my laptop with me so I can show the police all the articles on this doctor and the other facility he worked at.

I have everything I need and it is almost time to go. I put my shoes and coat on, then head down the hall to go to my car. I am stopped going out the door by the desk clerk asking me where I am going. I tell her I have a three hour pass and show her the paper signed by myself and Dr. Tom. She says, it is fine to go and to enjoy my time away. I go through the door leading to outside, and make my way to my car. I leave the facility and head to the police station. As I get about 5 minutes from the facility, I realize I forgot to take the pills I was saving. I need to show the police what they are giving me at that facility. They are not the pills I was on when I was admitted in here.

I find a place to turn around and head back to the facility. I need to go inside and get those pills I have in my room. I think every little bit of evidence will make this all seem real. I need the police to believe me. I park by the door and quickly go inside. I tell the desk clerk I need to get something out of my room. She just waves and says, "Okay", then down the hall I go. I get to my room and go inside to grab the little baggy of pills I have been saving.

I rush back to my car, which is parked by the door and I head to the police station. It doesn't take me long to get here and the parking lot at the police station is full of police cars. I gather up all my stuff and make my way inside. As I enter the station, I am greeted by Officer Smith. He recognizes me right away from the case involving the skeletal remains. He asks if I am here to see him for an update and I quickly tell him I have information on someone and need to speak to an officer about it. "I have time if you would like to come to my office and we can talk there," he says. I gladly accept and follow him down the hall to his office. I have my laptop and some papers with me.

Officer Smith tells me to take a seat. "How can I help you?" he asks. I begin by telling him I am at a facility and why I went there in the first place. I continue to tell him about how I was feeling after finding all the bodies in the cave and seeing the skeletal remains. "It really affected me. I was having nightmares and couldn't sleep at night. I stopped taking the pills shortly after getting there because I started to feel better. The nightmares even went away, so I started flushing them down the toilet. Then one day, I looked at it and it was not the original pill I was taking when I entered the facility. I then decided to save the pills in a baggy to show my doctor. That's when I began overhearing people at the facility talking about people dying there from drug overdoses." I then tell him about Dr. Tom and how he works there. I begin explaining that the other facility he worked at also had several deaths. I keep talking and talking so fast because I don't want to forget anything.

Officer Smith just sits and let me do all the talking. "Dr. Tom that works at the facility I'm at now, had a different name at the facility he worked at before," I say. I know I probably sound like I am talking in circles, but I continue with my story and my concerns. "I talked to the supervisor at the other facility. She told me that Dr. Tom was known as Dr. Ryan at her facility. So, he must be an imposter." I finish, finally taking a breath. I pull out my laptop and show Officer Smith the other facility and how his name is different at each place. I show him the article in the news paper about the deaths that happened at the other place Dr. Tom worked at. How he was acquitted because they had no proof and how the cause of deaths were all drug overdoses.

I ask Officer Smith if he can look further into this and possibly find other places Dr. Tom worked. *Maybe there is a connection somewhere. Has Dr. Tom been going from place to place and killing people off?* I wonder. He finds this to be very interesting and asks me how long I have been staying at the facility. I tell him I am better and just staying there now to keep an eye on Dr. Tom. I continue to tell him there has been 6 deaths at the facility since Dr. Tom started working there. All the deaths were drug overdoses, the same as the other facility. "How coincidental is that?" I ask. Officer Smith tells me that if this is true, then I can be in danger. *I can take care of myself and want to help the others before something happens to them,* I think.

"Can I keep the pills so I can send them to the lab and have them analyzed?" he asks.

"Yes, you can have them," I say.

I think he's starting to believe me and wants to follow up on this. *What if I am on to something?*

Officer Smith gets up from his chair and says he will be right back. He is gone for about 15 minutes and arrives back with an investigator. The investigator introduces himself as Jim Davis.

Officer Smith briefs him on the information I brought in and wants to get his professional opinion. Mr. Davis is quite impressed and wants to further investigate this. "It could be nothing, but you might be on to something here" he says. All 3 of us sit and go over the information I have about this so-called Dr. Tom. It really doesn't make sense for this Doctor to be using different names and why are so many people dying at facilities he worked at? They know they need to look further into this.

We talk until about 3:30 and I tell them I am just out on a 3-hour day pass and need to get back to the facility. If I am late, they may not let me take another day pass again. I give them both my cell number and tell them to call me anytime with information they may get. I also tell them I will be keeping an eye on Dr. Tom in the facility. They tell me to be careful and safe.

I leave all the paperwork and my pills with them. I take my laptop and head to my car to drive back to the facility. It is a quick drive back and a beautiful day. I want to go back to the cabin but I know this is the only way to get to the bottom of this. I don't want anyone else getting hurt so if this is what it takes, then I will stay longer. I get back to the facility and go directly to my room. I put my laptop away and get washed for supper. I am hungry and tired. My heart is racing thinking about my day at the police station. I kept looking in my rear-view mirror all the way back to the facility from the police station, in case I was being followed. I knew I wasn't, but my heart is still racing.

I head to the kitchen just before 5:00 to get a seat and wait for supper to be served. I can smell the fish cooking as I walk down the narrow hall. When I get to the kitchen there are no empty tables to sit at. Gail, a girl I met while staying here, waves to me to go sit with her. I go over to say hi and sit at the table with her.

"Where have you been, I haven't seen you in a while? I thought you might have left without saying goodbye to me," she says with a smirk.

"Oh, No, I just like to spend time alone and keep to myself" I tell her.

A few minutes later the kitchen staff start serving supper. We get up from the table to join the line for supper. As we get closer, we each grab a plate so we can be served. I tell Gail I love fish, but she doesn't like fish at all. We each get served our supper, which is fish, potatoes and corn. We are also allowed to take a bread roll if we want. I am starving so I take whatever they give me and a bread roll. Gail and I go back to the table to sit and eat. Gail puts her piece of fish on my plate. "Enjoy the extra piece of fish," she says with a smile. She tells me I can use the extra food because I am too thin. We both laugh and continue to eat. It is delicious but I am also very hungry. I eat everything on my plate, including the extra piece of fish from Gail. As I finish my food, Gail gets up from the table to get us both dessert. The dessert tonight is strawberry shortcake. Another one of my favorite foods.

We both finish eating our dessert and sit for a few minutes to talk. Gail asks me back to her room to watch tv or play cards.

"Do you know how to play crib?" I ask her.

"Yes! I love to play crib." She responds excitedly.

We take our plates up and put them in the large containers that are there for the dirty dishes. We leave and Gail wants to stop at the games room to get a crib board and cards. I tell her to go to her room and I will meet her after I brush my teeth.

It is now about 6pm, and I make my way to Gail's room to play crib. We laugh and joke while playing crib. It is the first time in a long time I have had fun like this. Gail trusts me enough to tell me why she is staying in the facility. She tells me her husband is having an affair with her best friend and he left her for the friend. "I was devastated and wanted to hurt myself" she says. "My family stepped in and got me the help and support I needed." She now realizes that he isn't worth it and is better off without him. She tells me the staff at the facility helped her with coping skills and made her feel whole again. She is staying one more week and then she will be leaving to go back home and start over.

We talk a little about myself and why I am in the facility. I tell Gail I am hopefully ready to be able to leave in the next couple of weeks. "I just have a few more things to work on before I go back home. I want to be strong enough, so I don't have to come back here ever again," I say. She agrees and says she needs to go home and get back to work. Getting back to work will get her mind off what happened. We are both yawning and realize it is after 9pm. We finish our game of crib and I tell her I think it's time to head back to my room.

I leave Gail's room and walk down the narrow hall to mine. I know the staff will be bringing my pill at 10pm so I want to be in my room when they arrive. I get in my pyjamas, crawl into bed and watch the news until I hear a knock on my door.

"It's Dr. Tom with your pill" he says.

"Come in" I respond.

He comes in, hands me my pill, then watches me take it. Afterwards, he says good night and leaves the room. I spit the pill out and put it in a new baggy. I had a long day and I am very tired. I had so much fun playing crib and won 4 out of the 5 games we played. Gail and I had a lot of laughs and she said she is starting to be back to her own self again. It is almost midnight and time to shut the tv off and get some sleep.

I am woken up at about 3am to a noise in the hallway. I can hear people outside my door but can't hear anything they are saying. I get out of bed and slowly open my door to look. I see Dr. Tom and another worker I haven't seen before. I think maybe he is a staff that only works the night shift. I can see the other worker on the phone. It sounds like he is talking to the police. I hear him tell the police his name is Eddy and to come right away. I know by the sound of his voice that this isn't good.

I keep my door open slightly and try to listen to what they are saying. I can hear the worker ask Dr. Tom how this happened but can't hear his response as he is further away from my door. A few minutes later, I see 2 police officers walk down the hall. They stop and are talking to Dr. Tom and Eddy, the other worker. They are in the hallway not far from my door. I hear the officer ask Dr. Tom what happened. The worker didn't wait for Dr. Tom to speak. Eddy began to tell the police he went into the patients room to do a room check and found him on the floor beside his bed. "I checked his pulse and he had no pulse" Eddy says. "He wasn't breathing and was cold. I immediately left the room to go find Dr. Tom."

The police officers ask Dr. Tom and Eddy to take them to the patients room so they can try to find out what happened. Dr. Tom and Eddy lead the way as the officers follow both to the room where the patient is still lying on the floor. It is close to me and I can see one of the officer's feet on the ground. I assume he is checking for a pulse.

"The patient is deceased. We will need to seal this room off until we further investigate and call for the coroner to come" says the officer.

"He died of NATURAL CAUSES" says Dr. Tom pretty loudly.

"Well, we don't know this for sure, so this is considered a crime scene until we investigate further" replies the officer.

Both officers ask them questions of who else is working at the facility tonight and what time the last room check was. The officer is writing everything down. He takes their names and continues asking questions about the patient. The officers want to know when the deceased checked into the facility and for what reason he was here. After about 30 minutes, the coroner arrives to remove the body from the room.

"We will be a little while" the officer tells the coroner.

"We have lots of time and can stick around. I will just tell my staff who are here to help me transport the body," the coroner responds.

After about an hour, the officers are done in the room. Everything is gathered and taken out for analysis. Fingerprints are taken off the door handles and one of the officers is carrying a bag with what looks like some sort of fibers. "Okay, guys you can remove the body now" says the officers.

I can hear one of the officers tell the worker and Dr. Tom, they will be in touch tomorrow if they have anymore questions. "The body will need to be sent out for an autopsy to get the cause of death" says the officer.

Dr. Tom and the worker follow the 2 officers to the door. I close my door and can't help but think, whether or not Dr. Tom has anything to do with this. I need to speak with Officer Smith but I will have to wait until the morning to call. I crawl back in bed and by this time it is 5am. I need to try to get a couple more hours of sleep. I am so thankful I went to the police station to report what I found out about Dr. Tom. This might make Officer Smith realize there is something strange going on here. I hope now that what I told Officer Smith will convince him to investigate this before more people die. Dr. Tom sounds like a real basket case and he should be the one in this ward. He is the sick crazy man doing all this to innocent people. I hope they throw the book at him and he spends the rest of his life in jail.

I toss and turn until 7am, before getting up and heading to the kitchen for a coffee. There is no way I can go back to sleep after the night I had. I will wait until about 9am to call the police station and talk to Officer Smith. I am hoping the news got back to the station and Officer Smith has already heard about the death at the facility.

I am sipping my hot coffee as I hear people in the hallway. I slowly and quietly open my door to get a look at who is there. I can see Dr. Tom and Eddy go in the room where the body was found. I don't know who it was that was staying in that room, so I have no idea who passed away. This place is giving me the creeps. If you are not crazy coming in, you will be crazy going out. I need to get out of here but need to get to the bottom of this. A few minutes later I can here someone else walking down the narrow hallway. I take a peak out my door and there stands Officer Smith. He is heading in the room where Dr. Tom and Eddy are. I can hear muffled voices, but have no idea what they are saying.

I don't want Officer Smith to leave before I get to see him. I get dressed in a pair of sweats and a t shirt then head out into the hall. I haven't I even brushed my hair. I need to talk to Officer Smith without anyone seeing us talk. I am hoping he will find a way to signal me to talk, or that I can find a way to tell him we need to talk.

I walk up and down the hall a few times and the door to the room where the body was found is shut. I just have to wait until Officer Smith comes out to see what he has to say. I am thinking I will just say hi and continue walking away, then call him when he leaves the facility. I don't want to raise suspicion with anyone about me talking to the police.

After about 30 minutes, Dr. Tom, Eddy, and Officer Smith come out of the deceased man's room. I can hear Officer Smith say they will be investigating this and are waiting on results from the autopsy. Eddy looks very upset that this happened. Finding a body when you enter a room isn't something you will forget. Dr. Tom walks to his office and Eddy walks to the front desk.

Officer Smith has a quick minute to ask me if I saw anything and I tell him I woke at 3am to Dr. Tom and Eddy in the hallway.

"I overheard Eddy say when he went in to do a room check, he found the body on the floor. Dr. Tom went in to check on the body and they both came out of the room, then police arrived shortly after that. Eddy seemed to be upset but Dr. Tom didn't flinch," I answer.

We can hear someone coming down the hall, so Officer Smith says he will be in touch later today. It is safer if we aren't seen talking together. I walk away and head to the kitchen to get toast and peanut butter. I am over tired and need to sleep but there is no way I can sleep now. I eat my toast and get a glass of orange juice to take it to my room. I want to change out of my sweatpants and put on a pair of jeans in case I need to go to the police station to talk to Officer Smith.

I figure it is going to be a long day and I probably won't hear from Officer Smith today. I stay in my room for a few hours. There is a knock on my door at 10am.

"Who is it?" I ask.

"It's Anne and I have your morning pill," she replies, with a soft voice.

"Come in" I say.

She enters my room and hands me my pill.

"Who does all the ordering of the medication?" I ask before taking my pill.

"Dr. Tom does all the medication for the facility. He told all of us staff that he likes doing it to keep busy," she answers.

"That's so nice of him" I say, taking the pill with my orange juice I got from the kitchen earlier.

Anne doesn't mention anything that happened last night. She looks like she has something on her mind and is distracted. She says goodbye and leaves the room. I take the pill out of my mouth and put it in the baggy I have. I stay in my room until lunch time and then make my way down the hallway to the kitchen.

I meet Gail in the hall and she asks me if I heard about the death last night. I tell her I did but wasn't sure who it was.

"His name was Chad and he has been in the facility for over a month" she says.

"Maybe if I saw a picture, I might have seen him in the hall or the kitchen," I tell her.

Gail tells me he spent most of his time in his room and the staff would bring him his meals. "He only left his room if he wanted to join one of the meetings but I only saw him do that twice, she says.

Gail and I make it to the kitchen to have lunch. We get in the line and grab a tray. The lunch today is a bacon cheeseburger and chicken salad. Gail orders a bacon cheeseburger and I get the chicken salad. I didn't realize it was a chicken salad sandwich and not a chicken salad. I'm a little disappointed, but it doesn't matter what it is because I am hungry. We sit at a table close to the window where we can look outside and see the sunshine. I eat my sandwich and Gail enjoys her bacon cheeseburger. She wants to go get another one but decides she doesn't really need it. She did go back up to the counter and get apple pie for dessert though. She loves her dessert. She asks me if I want dessert and I tell her "No thank you."

We are both done our meal and take our trays up to be cleaned. We leave the kitchen and head down the hallway. Gail asks me if I want to play crib, but I say I will play after supper. I tell her I want to go to my room to get some rest. We say goodbye and head to our rooms.

I get to my room and go inside before shutting the door behind me. I can't help but think Dr. Tom has something to do with these deaths. Anne has just told me Dr. Tom does all the medication for the facility. This can be the break we have been waiting for but we still must prove it. I need to talk to Officer Smith and let him know what I have just found out about the medication. I sit on my bed and grab a notebook to write a few things down, so I can go over everything with Officer Smith. I like to make sure I have dates and times, so it is more accurate.

I reach for my phone to check the time and realize I have a message. I listen to the message, which was left by Officer Smith at 12:30pm. He informs me that he has some information and needs to talk to me. He asks if I can meet him at the station this afternoon. I immediately call him back. I have his direct line, so I can call him without having to go through the front desk. As the phone rings, he picks it up as if he is waiting for my call.

"Officer Smith speaking," he says, answering the phone.

"Hi, this is Jill just returning your call," I tell him.

"Do you think you can get away for a meeting with me down at the station?" he asks me.

"I will have to find Dr. Tom and ask for another day pass. I don't think it will be a problem as I have had a few before. I will call you as soon as I have the day pass." I respond.

We hang up and I immediately get to work on getting my day pass. I leave my room and head down the narrow hall to Dr. Tom's office. I knock on the door, but he doesn't answer. I leave his office and go to the front desk where Anne is sitting. I stand, waiting as she is on the phone. She looks up to acknowledge me and I wait patiently until she is off the phone.

"Good afternoon, Anne, do you happen to know where Dr. Tom is?" I ask her.

"Dr. Tom is in a meeting and will not be available for awhile. Is there anything I can help you with?" she asks.

"Well, I would like a day pass to pick up a few items I need," I say.

Anne doesn't see a problem with giving me a day pass because she knows I've had a few before and there has never been an issue.

"It is getting late in the day. When would you like to go?" she asks.

"I would like to go soon, so I can get back for supper" I say.

She gives me a day pass from 2 to 5, tells me to try to be back for supper and to try not to be late. I head back down the hall to my room to get ready. It is almost 1:30, so I need to leave soon. I grab my cell phone and make a call to officer Smith.

"I got my day pass and will head to the station soon to meet with you," I say smiling when he answers the phone.

"That is great news! I will be waiting for you," he responds.

I take my purse and cell phone and make my way to the front door. I need to go back to my room and get my car keys I forgot on my table. I finally get back to the door and head outside to my car. The weather is beautiful and the sun is shining. All the things you miss when you are cooped up inside. I love being outside and this is the reason I need to get back home to my cabin and the outdoors. The traffic is slow moving, so it takes me a few extra minutes to get to the police station.

I get to the police station and walk through the doors, then make my way to the front desk. I tell the lady sitting at the desk that I am there to see Officer Smith. She gets up from her desk and says, "follow me, he's waiting for you"

We walk down a hallway and pass Officer Smith's office. I ask where we are going, and she says "to a conference room." I don't say anything else and continue following her. She knocks at the door and we hear, "come in." She opens the door and ushers me inside. Officer Smith stands up and introduces 4 other men sitting at a large table with high back padded chairs. After introducing me to the men sitting here, he asks me to take a seat.

The 4 men sitting in the room with myself and officer Smith are detectives. They say they are now investigating the deaths at both facilities. One of the detectives whose name is Jamie, does most of the talking. Jamie continues to tell me that the pills I handed in to be sent to the lab, came back with a trace of poison in them that slowly kills you. I am in shock, but not surprised. I am glad I stopped taking them and saved them to be examined. Jamie continues to say that they are investigating Dr. Tom at other facilities he has worked at over the years. They found 3 other facilities Dr. Tom has worked at in his 15 years and there were deaths at all of them. He has also used several different aliases.

"We are waiting on the latest autopsy report to see if there is trace of poison in his system" says Jamie.

"This is going to take some time and this is where we need your help," Officer Smith adds.

They are trying to put all the pieces together in a fast but professional way so nobody else gets hurt. They need to make sure they have enough evidence to put Dr. Tom away for life. I ask Jamie if they have pictures of Dr. Tom at the other facilities using a different name.

"We have everything in order along with the proof," Jaime replies.

"We just need to nail this son of a bitch," Officer Smith states angrily.

"How do I help?" I ask.

"Are you able to get access to Dr. Tom's office without getting caught?" Jamie asks me.

"I am sure I can. He never locks the door when he leaves," I say.

"I think it is too soon to get a search warrant without more evidence, but I will try my best. We need to move fast to avoid another death," he tells me.

"We don't want anyone else getting hurt but we need all the info we can get on Dr. Tom, so it's not thrown out of court this time," says Officer Smith a bit calmer now.

Jamie tells me what to look for if I can sneak safely into Dr. Toms office without getting caught. He wants me to look around for any pictures or notes with names or dates of anything out of the ordinary. Anything on the other facilities stating he worked in other places would be beneficial as well. "We are looking for some type of journal or a place Dr. Tom would write notes down on the names of victims. It is likely he kept a diary or logbook as a trophy or momentum," Jaime informs me.

"We need to find this," Officer Smith adds, with a concerned tone.

I agree to help them in anyway possible to get to the bottom of this. Jamie briefs me on how to be safe and ways not to get caught. He asks me to keep everything we talked about between only the people in this room. I tell him I agree and have no problem with that. "We need to get this crazy man and put him in jail where he belongs" I say.

Officer Smith speaks about how he had a conversation with Dr. Tom after the last death.

"I had the creepy feeling that Dr. Tom thought the young man was better off dead than alive" he says. "He doesn't seem like he cares at all, that there was a body found. He mentioned the young man was suicidal and finally got his wish to die," Officer Smith finishes.

He knows this isn't normal for a doctor who is supposed to help people.

"I have a thought after hearing what Officer Smith just said. W*hat if, Dr. Tom is killing off people who are suicidal, to give them their wish?*

What if he thinks he is doing them a favor, instead of trying to help them get better?" I state towards everyone in the room.

Jamie looks up from the table.

"That's a great thought. Maybe we are looking at this all the wrong way. What if Dr. Tom really thinks he is doing them a favor by killing these people off to take them out of their misery? We need to start looking into all the records of everyone that has died in every facility Dr. Tom worked at. We must find out if there is any connection with all these deaths," Jaime answers intrigued.

Officer Smith starts to realize I am on to something and this starts to make sense. Not that any of this makes sense for a doctor to kill people if they are suicidal. It is getting late, and I need to get back before 5:00. I don't want to be late in case I need another day pass. I tell Office Smith that I must get back to the facility and I will be in touch as soon as I have any information. He tells me to be careful and be safe.

I leave and head back to the facility in time to have supper. I get back and go inside to make my way down the hall to my room. I don't see anyone sitting at the front desk, but I do see a few people in the hall heading to the kitchen. I go to my room and put my things away, then get washed for supper. I didn't realize how hungry I am until I got to the kitchen and smell the food cooking. I notice Gail sitting alone so I go over to her table to join her. She smiles as I sit down.

"Where have you been all day?" she asks with a smile.

"I had a day pass and went for a drive to check on my cabin." I tell her.

"Oh, that's nice," she says.

The kitchen staff start serving the food, so Gail and I stand up to get in line. We each take our own tray and start down the line until we reach the ladies serving the supper. It is baked chicken with mashed potatoes and gravy. There is a side of glazed carrots and cranberry sauce as well. It smells so good. I ask for an extra scoop of potatoes. The kitchen staff gives me 2 large scoops and lots of gravy.

Gail and I get our supper and go to our table to eat. It is delicious but filling. I eat so much, that I think I am going to blow up. Gail doesn't eat as much as me and asks me where I put it.

She says, "you are so tiny and eat so much."

I tell her "I love potatoes and they make me feel full."

She answers, "that's why you don't eat dessert often isn't it?"

"Yes," I say and we both laugh at the same time.

We get up from the table and take our trays up to be cleaned. Gail asks me to go to her room and play crib. I gladly accept and tell her I will meet her in her room in an hour. I go back to my room to change into my sweatpants and a tank top. It is hot in the building and it makes me feel sick. I watch the news for about a half hour and then make my way down the hall to Gail's room to play crib. I just needed time for my stomach to settle before I go beat Gail at a game of crib.

It is almost 7pm and I know Gail is waiting for me to get to her room. I walk down the hall and knock on Gail's door. "Come on in and let me beat you in a few games of crib" she says. We both laugh and say good luck to each other. Gail has the crib board and cards ready to play. I open a bag of chips and she puts the music channel on the tv to play country tunes. We have so much in common and get along so well. I know Gail will be heading home soon, so I want to spend time with her before either one of us leave. She asks me if we can be friends when we leave this place. I tell her most certainly and we exchange phone numbers. I live outside of town, but Gail lives closer to town. I tell her I go to town every few days so we can meet up for coffee and she thinks this is a great idea.

We play cards until after 9pm, but we are both getting tired and decide to make this the last game. I need to get back to my room and get ready for bed before my 10:00pm pill comes. We finish the game and say good night to each other. I leave and wander down the hall to my room. On my way to my room, I stop by the kitchen for a glass of orange juice to take with me. Anne is there getting a coffee to take to her desk. She asks me how my day went. I tell her I went for a drive to my cabin to get a few things I needed. She then says she will be coming to my room soon with my pill. I ask her where Dr. Tom is, and she responds with "he left for the night and will be back tomorrow morning."

I get back to my room and get ready for bed, then wait for Anne to come give me my pill. She is right on time at 10pm. I hear a knock on my door and tell her to come in. She hands me my pill and I swallow it with my orange juice. She says good night and leaves my room. I again, spit my pill out and put it in a baggy.

I start thinking I will go to Dr. Toms office tonight and have a look around. I know he isn't in the facility, and it is usually a quiet night with very little staff. I know I need to take the chance in case I don't get another one anytime soon. I need to wait until about 11pm before sneaking down the hall. I go in the washroom to brush my teeth then come out and sit on the bed to watch tv, until it is time. My heart is racing but I know I need to do this to get some answers. We must nail this piece of crap.

I need to make sure everyone is in their rooms, before I make my way down the hall to his office. I don't want to get caught, because then I will have some explaining to do. I have a plan if I happen to get caught though. I will just say I couldn't sleep and wanted a book to read. Dr. Tom has a variety of them on his bookshelf and I wanted to borrow one. I leave my door open just to the edge so I can hear when the coast is clear. I need to make sure Anne is at the front desk and everyone else are in their rooms.

It is shortly before 11pm and has been quiet for about half an hour now. If I was going to do this, I must go now. I leave my room and quietly make my way down the hallway to enter Dr. Tom's office without being seen. As I start walking down the hall, I can hear someone cough in their room, so I quietly speed up. I need to get to the office before someone sees me and asks me what I am doing. I tiptoe as best as I can. My heart is beating and sounds so loud.

I make it safe, down the hall to the office and check to see if the door is unlocked. I take a deep breath and turn the handle to the door. It is unlocked so I go inside and shut the door behind me. My heart is racing. I know I can't put a light on, so I use the flashlight on my cell phone. I start to look around to see if I can find anything Dr. Tom might be hiding. I might not even know what I am looking for until I find it. It's harder in the dark than you think it is. I don't see any pictures on the walls and he doesn't even have a doctor certificate with his name on it. I keep looking around but I'm not having any luck so far. I decide to see if Dr. Tom might have something in his desk drawer. I look through some of the drawers that are on the side of the desk. He has some files and paperwork in the first 2 drawers and the bottom drawer is empty. I put the flashlight on some of the papers, but it is just files from people in this facility. I don't see anything that is of interest yet. I put all the files and paperwork back in the drawer and go to a drawer on the other side of the desk. This drawer is locked and I need to get it open. I don't want to break the drawer. Dr. Tom will know someone was in his office if I do that. I try and try, but there is no way this is going to open without something sharp to put in the keyhole. I look around and find a pair of scissors with a long narrow point. I think I will try them but need to be very careful I don't break the lock.

I need to be quiet and make sure not to scratch the wood on the desk. Finally, after a few minutes the lock turns and I pull on the drawer until it opens. I lye the scissors on the desk and start looking through the drawer. I find a stack of files and lye them on the desk. I start taking everything out of the drawer and when I reach the bottom there is a small wooden box. I take the box out and open it. I can't believe my eyes when I see what's in the box. I am looking at pictures of men and women with a line drawn through their faces in black marker. I don't know what this means, so I start taking pictures of the photos that I found in the box. I find a list underneath all the photos and beside each name says deceased. This doesn't prove anything yet. I need something concrete to incriminate Dr. Tom. I take as many pictures as I can of everything I find. I keep searching for more. We need to nail this guy.

At the bottom of the drawer is a stack of passports and a notebook. I start opening the passports to look through them. I count 6 passports in total. As I open each passport, I see a picture of Dr. Tom inside all of them. The one thing I notice, are that the pictures are the same, but they all have a different name on them. I put the passports on the desk and start looking through the notebook. I flip through the pages and there are names and dates of so many people. There are dates of when people died and newspaper clippings from all the deaths. This still doesn't prove he had anything to do with the deaths though. I keep flipping pages until I finally get to the middle of the book. In the middle of the book, it shows names and how many pills it took until their death. It goes on to say they are better off dead and that's why I had to kill them. The book also says "they were going to kill themselves anyway, so I did them a favor and did it for them."

I can't believe what I am reading. Dr. Tom is admitting he killed these people because they were suicidal, and they wanted to die. I can hear someone walking down the hall so I shut my flashlight off so I won't get caught. It must have been someone going to the kitchen. I wait until it gets quiet again and turn my flashlight back on to keep looking. I make sure I put everything back in the drawer except the notebook and all 6 passports. They are coming with me. I need to get the drawer locked and get out of Dr. Tom's office before I get caught. The drawer locks without a problem, so I grab the notebook and passports and head to the door. I take one last look around to make sure there is nothing out of place. I put the scissors back where I found them and get out, so I don't get caught.

I open the door ever so slightly and check to see if the coast is clear. I don't see anyone in the hall, so I quietly shut the door and leave. I head back to my room before someone spots me. I get to my room and go inside, then shut the door behind me. I am shocked at what I found in Dr. Tom's desk. I climb in bed and start looking through the notebook. I put my lamp on that is on my table by my bed. I start flipping through each page. I find a list of places Dr. Tom has worked over the years and it gives names of the facilities, but not the dates he worked there. I know the police can find out the dates of these places Dr. Tom worked at, so I don't' worry. I continue looking through all the notes and keep reading and reading. I glance at my phone and am shocked to see that it is 2am I need to shut the lights out and get some sleep before it is daylight. I put the notebook and the passports underneath my mattress until morning.

I wake up at 8am, which is later than usual. I get washed, dressed and go to the kitchen for a cup of coffee. I decide to take the coffee back to my room and sit on my bed. I drink the coffee, which is very strong. It must have been made a while ago and just sat in the pot. I don't care though, and just drink it. I know it will wake me up. After I finish my coffee, I put the notebook and all 6 passports in my purse. I need to call Officer Smith and tell him I need to see him today.

I hear some noise in the hallway, so I quietly open my door and peak out. It is Dr. Tom and Anne talking about how the night went. I can hear Anne tell Dr. Tom that it was a quiet night. He finishes talking and makes his way down the hall to his office. I am hoping when he goes inside his office, he doesn't notice anything out of place.

I need to get another day pass to go to the police station to see officer Smith so I can give him the notebook and the passports. I put the tv on and try to pass the time. I know my pill is coming at 10am and I need to be here for that. At about 10:05, there is a knock at my door.

"Come in" I say. Dr. Tom walks in.

"How are you doing and how was your night?" he asks.

"I am fine but would like to have a day pass to go to the cabin to get some personal items," I ask.

"Come see me after 11am and I will have one ready," he responds.

I take my pill as he watches me and then he says goodbye before walking out, leaving the door open. I spit my pill out and put it in the baggie.

I go to the kitchen to get a cup of coffee and take it back to my room. I wait in my room until 11am and then go down the hall to see Dr. Tom and get my day pass. His door is shut, so I knock. "Come in," he says. I ask him if my day pass is ready and he says yes. I sign it and leave the office. I can go from 1pm to 4pm. Its important for us to be at the facility during mealtime. I head back to my room to call Officer Smith and let him know I have some documents he needs to see. I call his direct line, but there is no answer, so I leave a message for him to call me back. I also let him know that I am going to be at his office at about 1:30 with some documents.

I watch tv until it is time to go to the kitchen for lunch. I head down the hall to the kitchen just before noon. Gail is already sitting at a table and waves for me to come over. The lunch smells so good and I am hungry. Gail tells me that we are having chicken pot pie. I let her know that it is one of my favorites. They start serving lunch and we get up to go in the line. It isn't very busy today for some reason. We get our food and go back to our table. The chicken pot pie is delicious. We also have fresh homemade bread rolls. Gail says dessert today is brownies with chocolate icing. I tell her she can have mine. I am too full from eating the chicken pot pie and fresh roll.

She asks me what I am doing today and if I want to play crib.

"I have a day pass and have a few things to do, so maybe another time or even later tonight" I tell her.

"If I can get a day pass, would I be able to come with you for a drive?" she asks me.

"OH! Yes, that would be great" I say with a smile.

I can't really tell her I am going to the police station with information on Dr. Tom, so I need to tell a little white lie. I tell Gail that I am going to visit a friend that needs to talk to me about a personal situation and I will take her another day. That way we can have a coffee and go for a drive. She says that would be great.

We both leave the kitchen and head down the hallway. We stand by my room and talk for a few minutes and I tell Gail I will play crib after supper tonight. "That would be nice and I will see you tonight" she says. I tell Gail I will pick up some snacks from the grocery store to have while we play tonight. I ask her what she likes and she says "just surprise me."

We go back to our rooms and I finish getting ready to go to the police station. I have everything to go and just counting down the minutes until I can leave the facility. It is 12:50, so I get the stuff I need to take and shut my bedroom door. I walk to the front desk to tell them I am going on a day pass. I show them the signed paper by Dr. Tom and I leave the building as fast as my little feet will take me.

I get in my car and head to the police station. I listen to country music until I pull into the parking lot. I grab all the documents, so I can show Officer Smith what I found, in Dr. Tom's office. I am hoping this will be enough to put him away for a very long time. I get inside and tell the lady at the front desk I am here to see Officer Smith. She recognizes me from previous visits and calls him. "He says he will be right out" she tells me. He comes to the front desk and asks me to follow him. We go down the hallway to his office and he says "take a seat," then he shuts the door behind me.

I tell him I was able to get into Dr. Tom's office last night and retrieve some things from a locked drawer in his desk.

"What did you find and did you have any trouble getting in and out of the office?" he asks.

"No, I went after everyone was in their rooms and Dr. Tom's office door was not locked," I say with a smile.

"The only problem I had was 1 drawer of the desk was locked, but I managed to open it with a pair of sharp scissors," I finish.

I hand the documents to Officer Smith and he starts looking through everything. He can't believe what he is seeing in front of him. His eyes are wide open and he is just amazed at what I have found. He carefully reads the notes in the notebook and says "I think we have everything we need to arrest this man." He gets up from his chair and tells me he will be right back. He leaves the office and comes back after about 10 minutes with Jamie, the investigator who is working on the case. He pulls up a chair and asks Jamie to take a seat and hands him the notebook.

Jamie starts reading and flipping through page after page. "We got him now, that son of a bitch," says Jamie. He looks at all 6 passports and they all have Dr. Tom's picture, but all have a different name. They thank me for all my help but make me sign a nondisclosure agreement (NDA). I ask them if what I did was legal. Jamie informs me the judge allowed me to work with Officer Smith to solve this case. "We had found so many things that didn't add up with these deaths, so we got the judge to agree to sign a search warrant and use you to fulfill it. We told the judge it would be easier for you to access Dr. Tom's office from inside the facility. She was definitely on board with everything" says Officer Smith.

Officer Smith and Jamie, the investigator, say it will take a few days to get everything together to make the arrest of Dr. Tom. They also want to inform the judge of all the hard work I have done for them and how much it has paid off.

Officer Smith stands up and thanks me over and over for all my help. "We never would have solved this case if you hadn't come forward with the information" he says. Jamie also responds letting me know I was really brave and helpful with all the risks I took. He tells me I should be working under cover with the police to solve more cases. I tell Jamie and Officer Smith that if they ever need my help, they can call anytime. I get up and say I need to head back to the facility and that I am ready to leave this place for good. We all say goodbye and I head down the hall and out the door.

I leave the police station and drive to the grocery store to get some snacks. I have plans to beat my friend Gail in a few games of crib. I can't decide on a flavour of chips, so I get three different kinds. I also grab two chocolate bars and a bottle of root beer. I am so happy to be able to solve this case with the police and investigator. Hopefully this will save a lot of lives. I want to talk about it to my friend Gail, but I know I can't say anything. I just have to wait a few days and hopefully they arrest Dr. Tom. I don't want to leave the facility until I know he has been arrested. I am hoping to be at the facility the day the police come to arrest him.

I get back to the facility at 4:00pm, just in time for my day pass to end and head to my room to get changed, into a pair of sweatpants. I am getting hungry and can't wait for suppertime. I watch TV for a few minutes then hear a knock at my door.

"Who is it?" I ask.

"It's Gail," says a quiet voice.

"Come on in Gail" I tell her.

We talk a little about my day and how she is planning on winning when we play crib tonight. I just laugh and say, "maybe I will just let you win a game." She thinks this is funny. I tell Gail I picked up snacks for us and I show her what I got. She is really excited. It is just about 5:00, so we leave my room and head down the hall to the kitchen for supper. We both try to guess what we are having for supper tonight. Gail guesses Chicken and I guess fish. I tell her I like both, so it doesn't matter to me if it is one or the other.

We get to the kitchen and sit at the table we always sit at. We talk for a few minutes, until the kitchen staff say it is time to line up. We get up, grab a tray and get in line to be served. The supper tonight is shake and bake chicken with mashed potatoes. Gail laughs because she is right with her guess. We get our meal and sit back down at our table. The supper is delicious and I am so full after I eat. We get up from the table and take our trays back to be cleaned, then we leave the kitchen and head down the hallway to our rooms. I tell Gail I am going to my room to brush my teeth and grab the snacks, then I will be at her room to play crib.

After a few minutes of getting ready, I get the bag of snacks I bought and head to Gail's room. I don't want it to be a late night, so I go a little bit early. I had a long week and haven't gotten much sleep. I knock at the door and Gail tells me to come in. She has the crib board set up and I hand her the bag of snacks. We don't have any cups in the room for the pop, so I go to the kitchen to get a couple of glasses. When I get back, Gail opens a bag of BBQ chips and pours them onto a napkin. We play a few games of crib and eat some chips. She eats her chocolate bar, but I am still full of the big supper I had. I tell her she can have my bar. "Thank you!" she says.

We play crib until about 8:30, then I tell Gail I need to go to my room and get ready for bed. I am so tired. I just want to have a hot bath and get in my pyjamas. We say good night and that we will see each other in the morning for breakfast. I head down the hall and go to my room. I close the door and run my bath water. I want to be ready for bed when they come at 10pm with my pill. I have a nice hot bath and get in my comfy pajamas. I watch some tv until someone knocks on my door at 10pm.

"It's Dr. Tom with your meds" he says. He comes in and hands me the pill, then watches me take it. "Have a good night," he says, as he leaves my room. I take the pill out of my mouth and put it in the baggie. I don't think I really need to be saving them now, but I do just in case.

I climb in bed after Dr. Tom leaves and it doesn't take me long before I fall asleep. I wake at 2am to go to the bathroom and I fall back to sleep until 6am. I have a great sleep and I am ready for the day. I am hoping Officer Smith will come by today to arrest Dr. Tom, because I just want to go home; however, I need to see him get arrested first. I think I will sleep better knowing Dr. Tom is behind bars.

I get up and brush my teeth, then turn the tv on. It is too early to go to the kitchen for breakfast, so I just watch tv until it is time to go meet Gail. At about 8:30 I get dressed and make my way to the kitchen. At about 8:50, Gail strolls into the kitchen and sits with me. We talk for a few minutes then get up from the table to get in the line for breakfast. I can smell the bacon and eggs. I order 2 poached eggs over medium and rye toast. Gail gets bacon, eggs and 2 toast.

We are sitting down at the table eating when we hear some commotion in the hallway. We can hear noise and people arguing, so we get up to look. We peak out into the hallway and can see Dr. Tom in handcuffs. He is being escorted down the hall.

I recognize the officer leading Dr. Tom away in handcuffs right away. Officer Burns hasn't changed his looks at all, since the last time I saw him. I want to go say hi, but Gail is with me and no one is supposed to know that I helped them catch Dr. Tom. He sees me looking and he gives me a half smile and a nod. *Hopefully we will have a chance to talk. It has been so long since I've seen him,* I think to myself. This is one of the happiest days of my life, because I know I can finally go home. I tell Gail I don't want to finish my breakfast because I am not feeling well, and need to head back to my room. "I hope you feel better soon" she says. I leave, but instead of going towards my room, I make my way to the door to see Officer Burns putting Dr. Tom in his police car. I just need to see this happen, so I can get relief and closure. *We got that son of a bitch! We got that son of a bitch!* I think to myself as I'm jumping for joy on the inside. He closes the back door and goes to open the driver door when he notices me. Walking towards me, he signals Officer Smith, who walks over and gets in the driver side instead. I am a little surprised by the way Officer Burns now carries himself. He's more assertive and didn't need to say anything for Officer Smith to understand what he was asking of him. I feel instant relief watching Dr. Tom drive away in the back of the police car.

"Officer Burns!" I say as he walks towards me.

"Not quite. I'm Detective Burns now," he responds.

"Oh wow! Congratulations. I was wondering why I hadn't heard from you." I laugh surprised.

"I apologize that we lost contact. I was unable to keep in contact when they sent me away to train as a detective. It has been a very long road, but rewarding road. It's nice to see your natural instincts have continued to aide investigations. I have come across your name when working confidentially on several recent cases. It would be nice to continue that conversation regarding your help that we had so long ago. If your interested, that is." he asks.

"Absolutely I am!" I say smiling excitedly.

"Very well, I will have Officer Smith get in touch with you and he can handle the process. Nice seeing you Jill, take care." he tells me.

"You too!" I say as he turns and walks away, heading to his police car.

I feel relieved it is finally over and now I can get back to a normal life. I head back to my room and start to pack all my stuff so I can check myself out. I have to make sure I have everything, because I don't want to come back here ever again. It doesn't take me long before I have everything packed in a pile by the door of my room. I have one stop to make before I leave this facility. I have to go say goodbye to Gail. She is shocked I am leaving so soon. I tell her as soon as she gets home, she can call me anytime and we can meet for coffee. We have each others phone numbers now so I look forward to it.

I go back to my room, grab my stuff and head to the front desk. Anne is here and I tell her I am ready to leave. She says, "I think you are ready to leave too, but first you need to sign a few papers." She hands me everything to sign and when I'm done, she tells me good luck and gives me well wishes.

I get out the door and do a HAPPY DANCE! I run to my car and don't look back, then I drive and sing all the way home. I am happy to be finally be able to have a good night sleep in my own bed. It has been way too long since I had a good night sleep. I get in the cabin and unpack all my stuff, then put everything away. It doesn't take too long to get settled back in. I call my family and tell them I am home and doing well.

I know this is going to be an early night, but I need to have a coffee and sit on the deck. I miss this the most about the cabin. It's one of my favorite things to do when I'm at home. It is still early, so I relax and reminisce about everything in my life.

It is early afternoon when I decide to call Officer Smith to let him know I am at home and back to my healthy self. I call his direct line, but he doesn't answer, so I decide to leave him a voice mail. I know he will call me back as soon as he can. I walk around my property to get some fresh air. It feels so good to be home. I got a little spoiled in the facility having all my meals made. I wasn't used to that at all. Now that I'm home, I need to start cooking my own meals again. I love to cook and bake because it keeps me busy and passes the time.

I go inside the cabin to make a tuna sandwich and a cup of tea, then I sit down in my chair with my food and put the TV on. I watch a show and then the news comes on—it starts talking about Dr. Tom being arrested. The report says he has been charged in connection with several murders in several different facilities he had worked at, over the span of several years using different names. They say they have a notebook he kept with proof and 6 passports were also found in his desk drawer under lock and key. The news says it is an ongoing investigation and Dr. Tom will remain in jail until his trial. I am shocked to see this on the news so soon, but I guess they have enough evidence to make the arrest and go public.

I finish eating my supper when my phone rings. I answer my phone and it is Officer Smith returning my call.

"I am glad you are back home" he says.

"I am happy to be home and glad I was able to help you put that monster away. I am currently watching the news story on Dr. Tom," I tell him.

"We have enough evidence against him to put him away for a very long time," says Officer Smith.

He says they aren't done with him yet and they still have several more facilities to investigate before trial.

"This will hopefully add more years to his sentencing and he will spend the rest of his life behind bars where he belongs," he informs me.

"I agree, he should never see the light of day," I respond.

Officer Smith says he talked to Detective Burns and Jamie, who is the investigator on the case. They wanted to know if I am interested in helping them work on some other open cases. They say I did such a good job and was very accurate, along with follow directions with precision. Jamie told Officer Smith they could use someone like me in many cases that require a person to fit in and be trusted. "There are many courses you can take that will help you be more efficient" says Officer Smith. There are some criminal courses to take and some law courses. This will help me know things that I can and can not do, which are required by law, in order for evidence to be accepted into court. There are many things to learn, because if your actions are not precise, you could find out later that the evidence you found cannot be used; all because you didn't take appropriate steps. Everything must be done by the book and there are courses to help you learn this. No one wants a suspect to walk because of actions that could have been avoided.

Officer Smith asks me if this is something I would be interested in. We will pay for any and all courses required. Although, some might require me to go out of town. I don't even hesitate when I say yes. I would love to help and I am willing to take whatever courses they offer me. I think, *this is my chance to do something I always wanted to do.*

"Come by the station tomorrow to meet with Jamie and me to get things worked out. We will get you signed up for some courses being offered."

"I am super excited, and will see them at 10am." I tell him.

"Great! We will be waiting for you" he responds.

I say goodbye and just sit in my chair thinking, *this is going to be so exciting!* Working with law enforcement is going to keep me busy and maybe help get some criminals off the streets. I make a coffee and go out on the deck to get some fresh air. It is a beautiful evening, but I am still tired from all the sleepless nights while staying in the facility. I need to catch up on some sleep, so I go back inside at about 8pm and get ready for bed. I feel exhausted and hope I can get a good night's sleep. I crawl into my bed, roll over and within minutes fall fast asleep.

I wake at 6am, finally feeling rested after sleeping in my own bed. I get up and make a coffee, then head out to the deck. I can hear the birds and think about how much I missed this sound, while staying in the facility. I just sit here for 2 hours and listen to the chirping of the birds. It is so peaceful and relaxing. I decide it's time to go inside and get ready to go to the police station. I need a few groceries, so I decide to head to town early, so I can get home right after the meeting with the officers.

After getting my groceries, I head to the police station. I go inside and the lady at the desk smiles and says "Hi! Officer Smith is in his office waiting for you." She recognizes me from being here before. I know the way to his office, so I just head down the hall. Officer Smith's door is open and Jamie is sitting in a chair. They greet me and Officer Smith says "come in and take a seat." I take a seat and Jamie starts talking about some courses that are available. They want to sign me up for them. They go over the ones available now and let me know that they are everyday from 1 to 4, for 2 months. After these are done, I will have to go out of town for a month to take a law course and learn all about doing things by the book. While taking that course, there is a self defence course being offered in the evenings.

"It will be like killing 2 birds with 1 stone. If you can handle doing both at the same time, you will be able to start working with us sooner" says Jamie.

"Sign me up for whatever you want me to take. I am in 100 % and will give it my all, I tell him."

Officer Smith and Jamie have a case they must get to and tell me they will be in touch in a few days to give me all the information on the course. "I will be waiting for your call" I say.

I know this means the next few months will be very busy for me. This means my exploring and my adventures are coming to an end.... At least for now.

OTHER TITLES FROM THIS AUTHOR

Printed in Canada